"What is the matter with you?" Leo spoke furiously.

"You think a few dinners and a show entitles you to a woman's body. When and if I have a lover I'll want a lot more than a couple of dates and into bed," Jacy flung back at him.

"My apologies. I forgot that all women have a price. But if it's marriage you're holding out for, don't hold your breath."

JACQUELINE BAIRD began writing as a hobby when her family objected to the smell of her oil-painting, and immediately became hooked on the romantic genre. She loves traveling and worked her way around the world, from Europe to the Americas and Australia, returning to marry her teenage sweetheart. She now lives in the north-east of England and has two grown-up sons. She enjoys playing badminton and spends most weekends with husband Jim, sailing their Gp. 14.

Books by Jacqueline Baird

Jacqueline Baird
Gamble on Passion

Harlequin Books

TORONTO • NEW YORK • LONDON
AMSTERDAM • PARIS • SYDNEY • HAMBURG
STOCKHOLM • ATHENS • TOKYO • MILAN
MADRID • WARSAW • BUDAPEST • AUCKLAND

ISBN 0-373-11726-4

GAMBLE ON PASSION

Copyright © 1994 by Jacqueline Baird.

First North American Publication 1995.

CHAPTER ONE

'QUIET, everyone.' Replacing the telephone receiver, Liz glared threateningly around the crowded lounge of her apartment. 'Ssh. That was the porter. Tom is on his way up.' Her glance rested on the attractive blonde standing by the door. 'Dim the lights, quick,' she commanded, pushing her way through the crush of people to join her friend.

Jacy switched off the light and glanced down at her hostess for the evening. 'Stand by for action,' she prompted reassuringly. Liz was petite, with short black curly hair and sparkling blue eyes, but tonight she looked decidedly nervous.

'Do you think he will be pleased at a surprise fortieth birthday party?'

'Liz, your husband worships you ·and the terrible twins; anything you do is great with him and you know it!'

'Yes, you're right—I hope... But what about our bet— are you still game?'

Jacy glanced around the crowd of partygoers assembled in the large, comfortable room, all friends of Liz and Tom. 'Of course I am.' She grinned. 'But in all fairness to you I should point out that, as all the guests have arrived and all the single men here are my friends, it's no contest. The first one to walk through this door will be the one I date for a month. I'm bound to win.'

Liz smiled mischievously. 'I don't mind. I'll take the chance if you will.'

'Shake on it, partner.' Jacy grasped her friend's hand, shaking it vigorously, and couldn't resist adding, smugly, 'The *netsuke* is as good as mine.'

The door swung open and Tom, a tall blond-haired man, strode into the room. 'What the hell——?'

The room erupted to the strains of 'Happy Birthday to You' as Jacy clicked the light back on, and she stopped singing in mid-note, her eyes widening in horror at the black-haired, dark-eyed man who walked in behind Tom. Oh, no, she groaned inwardly, it couldn't be... She tried to sidle backwards into the crush of people surrounding the birthday-boy, but in the enthusiasm of the moment, to her horror, she was pushed slap-up against the tall dark man she was hoping to avoid.

A strong arm curved around her waist, and dark brown eyes glittered knowingly down into hers. 'Hello, Jacy, you're looking good.' A cynical smile twisted the hard mouth. 'But I admit I didn't think your sort would be a friend of Tom and Liz.'

Jacy, numb with shock, managed to reply icily, 'I could say the same about you,' while registering the fact that the black eyes burning into hers did not look in the least surprised to see her here. She dismissed the thought as fanciful and pushed past him and out into the hall.

She closed the door of the dining-room behind her and fell back against it. Her legs were trembling and the beating of her heart sounded unnaturally loud in the quiet of the room. Her glance slid across the dining-table, groaning under the weight of all the food she had helped prepare earlier and had been looking forward to eating. Now she had no appetite at all.

Damn! she swore under her breath. What was Leo Kozakis doing here? The internationally known Greek tycoon, at Tom's party? A family birthday party was hardly his scene, she thought bitterly. She hadn't realised Tom even knew the man.

Briefly she closed her eyes and ten years of her life were swept away. She swallowed hard on the lump that rose in her throat, feeling once again all the old pain and heartache of her much younger self. At eighteen Leo Kozakis had almost destroyed her, and now once again he had appeared in her life. The last man on earth she wanted to meet.

Taking a deep breath, she straightened and crossed to the table. She was over-reacting, she told herself. So what if Leo was at the party? It didn't make any difference to her. She was no longer a naïve teenager but a mature, successful career-woman of twenty-eight. Tom and Liz were her friends, and there was no way she was going to allow the unexpected appearance of Leo to frighten her into walking out on their celebration.

An ironic smile twisted her wide mouth as she realised Kozakis had been the first unattached male to walk through the door. Well, that was it! She had lost the bet... There was no way she could date him for a month, or would even want to. It had been a stupid bet, but there was no escaping the fact—Liz had won. Jacy was going to have to spend eight weekends looking after Liz's twin five-year-old boys. Still, it was her own fault, and she didn't mind: she loved the two boys, and her social life wasn't that exciting anyway.

It had all started earlier that afternoon. Jacy had promised to arrive at three to help prepare the food for the party. Liz hadn't wanted to use caterers, saying it seemed wrong to throw a surprise party for her husband and then stick him with a huge bill. Planning on leaving the office early, Jacy had been delayed by her office junior, Barbara, crying her heart out. The man from the assessors' department whom the girl had dated since the office Christmas party three months ago had finally talked her into bed. Unfortunately Barbara had been dreaming of wedding-bells until today. At lunchtime the poor soul had walked into the local pub in time to hear two of the male members of the staff talking to her boyfriend, and money changing hands. Seemingly, the man had only taken her out for a bet. They had laid odds on how many weeks it would take to get her into bed.

Jacy had arrived at Liz's two hours late, fuming over what swine men were, and declaring that just *once* she would like to do the same to one of them. Plus, in a way, she blamed herself, as it had been she who had persuaded the girl to go to the office Christmas party, and encouraged her to mix socially with the rest of the staff. She had felt sorry for Barbara, fresh from the north of England and in her first job in London.

Liz had listened to Jacy's angry tirade and then said, 'Well, why don't you?'

Jacy would never have bet money, but Liz had been clever; she had known the one thing that would tempt her. Six years ago the two women had met for the first time at a country house auction. They had both been bidding for the same lot: a delightful ivory *netsuke* with unusual jade eyes. Jacy had a modest collection of the tiny figures and had set her heart on the tiny Buddha. But Liz had outbid her. After the sale Jacy had congratulated Liz, and the two girls had got talking. It was an unlikely friendship. Liz had never worked since her marriage a year earlier and was heavily pregnant with the twins, while Jacy was quickly climbing the career ladder as a loss adjuster with a large insurance firm.

The sudden upsurge in the music and laughter brought Jacy back to the present with a jolt. The party had spread to the hall, and in only moments she would be forced to face the crowd again and Leo Kozakis... She couldn't do it. Her stomach churned sickeningly, and it was only with the greatest effort of will that she managed to straighten her shoulders and pin a smile on her face as the dining-room door swung open. She relaxed slightly when she saw who it was.

'There you are, Jacy. I wondered where you had got to.' Liz, a smug smile on her pixie face, added, 'You lucky lady, did you see that Leo Kozakis? Aren't you glad you made the bet?'

'No! And you win. Just tell me which weekends you want me to babysit.'

Liz stood in front of her, her blue eyes narrowed on Jacy's sombre face. 'Come on, love, you can't chicken out now. In the six years I've known you you have never gone out with the same man more than a couple of times. What is it? Are you afraid you might discover you like men?'

'No, of course not, but...' How could she explain how she felt? Liz would never understand. She was a happily married woman with a loving husband who had a good position as the director of a merchant bank. They owned a house in Surrey, and this apartment in town. They adored each other, and their twin boys were icing on the cake. Whereas Jacy had been deeply hurt as a teenager and had vowed never again to get involved with a man. She had a good job and was thoroughly independent, and that was the way she liked it.

'I never had you down as a coward, Jacy,' Liz said bluntly. 'Let me introduce you to Leo; he really is a great guy. Tom brought him down to Surrey last weekend and I thought straight away that he was perfect for you.'

Jacy eyed Liz with growing suspicion. 'Wait a minute... Tom rang to say he was on his way up,' she murmured, and watched the elfin features of her friend colour a delicate red. 'You knew... You *knew* he was bringing that man when we shook on the bet.'

'*Mea culpa*,' Liz admitted unashamedly. 'But a bet is a bet, and he is gorgeous!'

'It's no good, Liz, you're wasting your time, for the simple reason that the man would never ask me out in a million years!' Jacy knew it was true, but she had no intention of telling Liz how she knew. Some things were too painful to discuss even with her best friend.

'Now you *are* being ridiculous.' Liz stepped back and surveyed Jacy from head to toe. 'You're drop-dead gorgeous, five foot five, gold hair, gold eyes, and that slip of a red sheath you're wearing clings to every luscious curve. Who are you trying to kid, pal? One flutter from those incredibly long eyelashes and the man will be kneeling at your feet. Your trouble is, you can't accept how attractive you are. Even my Tom said that when you walk across a room you're like a magnet, attracting every male eye in the place.'

'Flattery will get you nowhere, friend. Take it from me, Mr Kozakis will not ask me out, even if I were to strip naked in front of him.' Jacy was not aware of the bitterness edging her tone, or the questioning look the other girl gave her, as she continued, 'I may be a liberated female, but when we made the bet you did agree that I don't have to ask the man. He has to ask me, and in this case it will never happen. So tell me when you want your first free weekend, hmm?'

'Think of the *netsuke*, the exquisite Buddha, the jade eyes,' Liz tempted teasingly. 'A month dating Leo the Hunk wouldn't kill you, and I expect you to at least try and honour the spirit of the bet.'

Jacy never had a chance to answer, as a voice broke into their lively exchange.

'The two most beautiful women in the place.' Tom appeared beside his wife, curving an arm around her shoulders. 'But I should be angry with you, Liz; now everyone knows just what an old married man I am.' His blond head swept down, and he kissed his wife firmly before adding, 'Poor Leo here thought he was going to collect some papers and go.' Tom turned his sparkling blue eyes on Jacy. 'Jacy, let me introduce you to Leo, a business friend of mine. I want you to look after him and make sure he gets fed, while *I* deal with my scatty wife.'

Jacy forced a smile to her stiff lips. 'Happy birthday, Tom.' And, leaning forward, she kissed him lightly on the cheek, studiously ignoring the man at her side.

There was no way on God's earth she wanted anything to do with the arrogant Greek. But Leo had a different idea. Stepping in front of his host, he quite deliberately caught Jacy's hand in his before she could object and, moving closer, he flicked his dark eyes coldly over her flushed face.

'There's no need for introductions, Tom; Jacy and I are old friends. We met when she was a budding reporter.' Dropping her hand, he deliberately turned his back on her to speak directly to Tom. 'Though given the sensitive nature of some of your work I was surprised when you mentioned that Jacy, a journalist, was a family friend of yours...'

Tom threw his blond head back and burst out laughing, while Liz's inquisitive blue eyes darted from the Greek to Jacy and back again.

'Jacy, a reporter?' She grinned. 'You must have the wrong girl. Jacy is a very valued member of the Mutual Save and Trust Company. In fact, she's their top loss adjuster. She can smell a fraud a mile off.'

As far as Jacy was concerned, Leo Kozakis was the biggest fraud alive, she thought angrily; and what did he mean? He'd said, 'was a friend'. Had he known she would be here tonight? No, it was impossible; and at that moment her attention was caught by someone calling her name.

'Jacy, darling, I've been looking all over for you. I've got your G and T.'

Thank God for Simon, she thought gratefully, and with a mumbled, 'Excuse me,' she walked across to join the laughing crowd that had entered the dining-room.

'Thank you, Simon.' She took the proffered glass from the hand of the tall ginger-haired fresh-faced young man, and urged him back out into the hall towards the lounge. 'Let's find a seat and gossip,' she encouraged, shooting him a brilliant smile. She could have hugged him for getting her out of an intolerable situation, but she doubted it would be appreciated, as she was one of the very few people who knew that Simon's taste ran to members of his own sex rather than females.

They found a vacant armchair and Jacy sank down into it with a sigh of relief, and took a long swallow of her drink. 'You've no idea how much I needed that.' She turned her face up to look at Simon who was perched on the arm of her chair, with a glass of whisky in one hand and his other arm resting lightly along the back of the chair.

'I don't believe it. Jacy the ice-maiden actually ruffled; and by a man, if I'm not mistaken.' And, lowering his head, he whispered in her ear, 'You can tell *me* about it, Jacy; your secret is as safe with me as I know mine is with you.'

'Simon, don't ask me to explain, just stay with me for the rest of the evening.' She turned sombre golden eyes up to his. 'Pretend we're good friends.'

'I don't need to pretend, we *are* good friends; and don't worry, I'll shield you from the Greek.'

Her eyes widened in shock. 'How...?' She stopped herself, but it was too late.

'It doesn't take a genius to work it out. He's the only new male in this crowd, and gorgeous with it. I watched him myself when he walked in, but I could tell instantly that he's not for me, more's the pity.'

Jacy burst out laughing; she couldn't help it. The idea of Simon seducing Leo: now that really did appeal. Draining her glass, she settled back in the chair and prepared to be entertained by Simon's outrageous stories for the rest of the evening. But some inner radar told her the instant Leo Kozakis walked into the room. She couldn't actually see him from the depths of her chair, but she had the uncanny feeling he was watching her.

Someone put the stereo on and the centre of the room gradually filled with swaying bodies, and then she saw him; he was dancing with a tall blonde. Dancing wasn't the word, she thought disgustedly. The woman had her arms around his neck, and Leo's hands were settled intimately over the blonde's buttocks. Ten years hadn't changed him at all. He was still the lecherous swine he had always been.

He looked over his partner's shoulder, his dark eyes catching Jacy watching him; and to her chagrin his lips curved in a knowing smile. She felt the blood surge in her cheeks and quickly looked away. Years ago she had thought herself in love with Leo Kozakis. A few magical weeks on the island of Corfu; the sun, the sea and the sand; a vibrant, tanned male body...

Jacy drained her glass in one gulp, dismissing the memory from her mind. Of course it had only been a childish crush, and she had quickly recovered; but the hurt and humiliation still lingered. Abruptly getting to her feet, she caught Simon's hand in hers. 'Come on, Simon, let's find the bar and have another drink. Tonight I think I'm going to need it,' she concluded as with Simon's arm around her shoulder they circumvented the dancing couples to arrive at the makeshift bar set up in one corner of the lounge.

Grasping her second gin and tonic, Jacy deliberately kept her back to the room and drank the potent spirit much too fast. But she had the uncanny feeling that Leo

Kozakis's dark eyes were watching her, and that he was laughing.

'Take it easy, Jacy,' Simon remonstrated as she held out her empty glass for a refill. 'An hour or so and I'll take you home.'

'Get lost, Simon. I want to talk to my friend,' Liz's laughing voice interrupted.

Jacy sighed, and sipped her drink, eyeing Liz over the top of her glass. 'Lovely party, Liz,' she said politely, the warning in her dark golden eyes telling her friend more plainly than words that she was not going to discuss Mr Kozakis.

'Don't try and intimidate me with your best "claim refused" frown. I want some answers. A: when were you ever a reporter? and B: how did you meet Leo? And the biggy: were you an item? That will do for starters.'

Jacy's first thought was to refuse to answer. Then, whether it was the drink or because she had finally regained her self-control, she thought, Why the hell not? Liz was her friend and Leo Kozakis meant nothing to her.

'I was never a reporter: that was a particular misconception of Mr Kozakis'; something he is prone to. As for how I know him, I met him when I was eighteen and on holiday in Corfu for the summer. As for being an item, as you so crudely put it, Liz: what do *you* think?' she drawled scornfully, her glance slanting over the delicate features of her friend's face. Without noticing the warning look in her sparkling eyes, Jacy continued, 'Give me some credit! The man's affairs are legion and very well documented by the Press; the swine's reputation is as black as his hair.'

'Does that mean that now I'm going grey my reputation will improve accordingly?' a deep mocking voice drawled in Jacy's ear.

She swung around, the glass slipping from her hand, and with lightning reflexes it was caught by the man standing in front of her, only a few drops splashing on his immaculate business suit.

'I did try to warn you,' Liz murmured as she faded away into the crowd.

Jacy stood as though turned to stone, the colour flooding into her pale cheeks.

'No answer, Jacy; but then you always had the ability to remain mute when it suited you, I seem to remember,' he declared hardly. His dark eyes blatantly surveyed her, from the top of her head, where her long golden blonde hair was swept up into a coronet of curls, down over the swan-like arch of her neck to her bare shoulders. They lingered on the soft curve of her breasts, lovingly cupped by the smooth red velvet strapless bodice of her dress, and continued down to her narrow waist, the round curve of her hips, and the long length of her legs, exaggerated by the spike-heeled red evening sandals. 'I must admit,' he confessed, his dark glance flicking back to her flushed face, 'my memory of your delightful body does you an injustice. You have certainly matured into a stunning woman, Jacy.'

Recovering from her initial dismay at his intervention into the conversation, Jacy was doing some appraising of her own. She had forgotten just how shockingly masculine he was. His navy pin-striped jacket fitted perfectly over his wide shoulders, and the matching trousers, belted low on his waist, clung to his muscular thighs. Slowly she raised her head to look up into his handsome face. His pale blue silk shirt contrasted sharply with the bronzed skin. His mouth, the bottom lip fuller than the top, curled back over perfect white teeth in a mocking smile that as she tilted her head further she realised didn't reach the dark brown, almost black eyes. His black hair *was* going grey, she realised in surprise; in fact, two silver

wings brushed back from his temples. The shock of black
curls that she remembered falling over his broad forehead
were now cut fashionably short and were also liberally
sprinkled with grey. But then he must be almost forty.
When she'd first met him he'd been twenty-nine. Ten
years! It didn't seem possible.

'Sorry I'm not dressed for dinner, but will I pass?'
Leo demanded mockingly.

Pass? He knew damn well he would, Jacy thought bitterly. But it didn't stop her too-fair skin from betraying
her now as it had when she was a teenager. The blush
that had started on her pale cheeks suffused the whole
of her body. 'You can pass me by any time. In fact, I
would prefer it,' she managed to respond cuttingly, proud
of the cold tone in her usually husky voice.

'Now, is that any way to greet an old friend? A dance
would be *much* more acceptable.' And, before she could
protest, his strong arm had encircled her waist and his
other hand had put the glass back on the bar and caught
Jacy's slender hand to his broad chest.

A shudder skittered down her spine, and she stiffened.
'I do not *want* to dance,' she snapped; his arm around
her waist was like a ring of steel.

'You must, they're playing your tune, Jacy,' Leo
prompted, holding her away from him, his mocking
glance sweeping down her body and back to her flushed
face before pulling her into intimate contact with his virile
form.

The lively music had given way to 'Lady in Red', she
realised angrily; but unless she wanted to make a scene
in front of her hosts and all their friends she knew she
would have to endure dancing with the man.

Shakily she moved where he led, trying to still the insistent tremors inside her. What was happening to her?
Jacy thought wildly. She despised Leo Kozakis but, held
close to his hard body, with his strong hand holding hers

firmly to his chest, she felt an incredible urge to close her eyes and relax into him. Until he spoke.

'So, when did you give up the reporting?'

Jacy clenched her teeth and swallowed hard. She would not let him bait her, she vowed. She had never *been* a reporter; had never really seriously considered the idea. But her father had been an editor of an American tabloid, and that had been enough for the younger Leo Kozakis...

'What happened? Couldn't you compete with your father?'

'My father is dead,' she said flatly, persuading herself that the shiver from her hand in his to her arm and right through her body was pure anger.

'I'm sorry, I didn't know.'

Jacy tilted her head back the better to look into his dark face. Her strange golden eyes flashed angrily as they clashed with black. 'You're not sorry, you liar. You despised him.' She spat the word out, trying to ease herself away from the closeness of his overpowering male form; but he strengthened his grip on her hand, his arm around her back holding her tighter.

'I never lie. I *am* sorry for the death of any living being.' His dark eyes burnt into Jacy's. 'I didn't despise your father, only the rag he worked for. How could I hate him? I didn't know him personally.' His firm mouth relaxed into a smile. 'But you—*you*, Jacy, I did know very personally; or so I thought at the time.'

Jacy stiffened in his arms. 'Well, you thought wrong; you didn't know me at all,' she said icily, ignoring the sensual knowledge in his smile.

'Then perhaps we can rectify that. Have dinner with me tomorrow night.'

'Huh!' A surprised gasp escaped her. The conceit of the man was unbelievable. To casually ask her out to dinner when the last time they had met he'd called her

worse than a whore! The words were indelibly carved
into her brain. She could hear them again in her mind,
his voice icy with contempt as he told her, 'At least a
whore has the basic honesty to state a price. But women
like you turn my stomach. Your type bleed a man dry
before the poor sod even knows he's paying for it.'

Jacy hadn't responded to him then, and she didn't
now. A chilling coldness took possession of her body;
her golden eyes, strangely blank, stared up into his darkly
attractive face. 'No, thank you,' she said politely.
Conveniently for Jacy, the music stopped, and, pulling
her hand from his, she stepped out of his hold, adding,
'Thank you for the dance.'

'Wait!' His large hand once again closed over her arm
as she turned to walk away. 'Why not?' The question
brushed past her ear. 'I'm in town for a month, we could
have some fun.'

Jacy looked down at the long brown fingers encircling
her white flesh and had to fight down a shudder of dis-
taste. She raised her head and Leo moved in front of
her, blocking her escape.

'After all, Jacy, you're no longer a teenager but a
mature woman. Better still, you're not a reporter as I
thought. I can see no problem with our getting together
again for a while.'

The amazing thing was, Jacy realised, the man actually believed what he was saying. Her glance slid up
over his handsome face. It was all there: the sensual anticipation in his dark eyes, the self-satisfied smile curving
his generous mouth. He moved closer, his warm breath
touching her cheek.

'Liz told me that you're unattached at the moment,
so how about it?' He murmured the words against her
temple, his lips brushing her skin like softest silk. 'I can
still remember how great we were in bed together,' he
breathed throatily.

Later, Jacy was to ask herself again and again why she did it. Was it Liz's bet? Or was it the red haze of fury that engulfed her when Leo reminded her of their past intimate relationship?

CHAPTER TWO

LEO KOZAKIS was without doubt the most arrogant, insensitive male chauvinist pig it had ever been her misfortune to meet, Jacy thought furiously, rage bubbling inside her like a volcano about to erupt. She clenched her teeth and counted to ten under her breath before even trusting herself to speak to the man. How dared he remind her of the passion they had shared? And to assume that he could take up again where they had left off years ago, simply because he had a few weeks in town and she was no longer a threat as a would-be reporter...

How many women over the years had he used in such a cavalier fashion? Hundreds, if the newspaper stories about him were even half true. She thought of the poor young girl, Barbara, whom she'd spent over an hour trying to comfort that very afternoon. The girl had reminded her very much of herself at that age, and she wouldn't mind betting that Barbara's ex-lover was a carbon copy of Leo Kozakis, but without the incredible wealth.

Betting. The bet... Jacy pinned a smile on her lovely face and, tilting her head to one side, glanced up through her long lashes at the man in front of her. 'You want to take me out to dinner?' she asked coyly, and almost laughed out loud at the gleam of triumph that flashed in Leo's eyes.

'That and more, my sweet.' His lips brushed her brow, and she had to clench her fist to prevent herself from wiping his touch from her forehead. 'Name the time and the place, Jacy, and I'll call for you.'

'As it happens, I have a free evening on Saturday.' She didn't want to appear too eager, and a three-day wait would do the man good. Jacy had never considered herself a vengeful person, but the reappearance of Leo had awakened a lot of bitter memories and these, added to the bet she'd made with Liz, meant that she couldn't resist the temptation to try and deflate the overwhelming ego of the man. She vowed to herself that she'd date the swine for a month, win the bet, and Leo Kozakis would learn a lesson in patience and self-denial that he would never forget...

'Enjoying yourselves?' Liz appeared from behind Leo. 'I hope Jacy is taking care of you, Leo.' The petite woman's blue eyes sparkled happily as she stood between the tall, handsome man and her best friend.

Jacy watched as Leo, ever the charmer, turned his brown velvet eyes on his hostess; the man oozed charm from every pore. 'This is quite the best party I have ever attended, Liz; Tom is a very fortunate man, and yes, Jacy is looking after me beautifully. In fact she's just agreed to dine with me on Saturday night.' His glance slid back to where Jacy stood, his eyes gleaming with pure male satisfaction and something more... 'I couldn't be happier.'

A shiver of unease trickled down Jacy's spine: the challenge in his gaze as it rested on her face then slid provocatively down to her toes and back up again was unmistakable. He reminded her of some predatory jungle cat toying with its prey before finally devouring it completely.

'Yes, well——' she burst into speech, unconsciously taking a step away from Leo and nearer to Liz '—it's a lovely party, Liz, but if you don't mind I'll say goodnight.'

'But it's early, you c——'

'No, I must go,' Jacy cut in. She couldn't keep up the pretence much longer; suddenly she felt disgusted with herself, and even more so with Leo Kozakis. She could feel the onset of a tension headache and all she wanted to do was get home and forget tonight had ever happened. As for the dinner-date, it had been a stupid idea to look for revenge—especially with a man like Leo. 'Unlike you, Liz, I'm a working girl, and I have a busy day ahead of me tomorrow, so if you'll excuse me I'll call a cab...'

'That won't be necessary: I'll take you home,' Leo offered smoothly.

'What a great idea!' Liz beamed. 'I hate the thought of my best friend travelling around London on her own at night.'

Jacy could have quite happily flattened Liz, and she deliberately ignored her friend's wink and thumb in the air, out of sight of Leo.

'No, please... Leo must stay. I'll be OK.'

Ten minutes later, sitting in the passenger seat of a sleek black Jaguar car with Leo Kozakis at the driving-wheel, she heard herself giving him her address in Pimlico.

'Why do I get the feeling you were somewhat reluctant to let me drive you home?' Leo cast her a sidelong glance before returning his attention to the road. 'Odd, when you've agreed to dine with me.'

Jacy frowned, her golden eyes flicking to his dark profile and away again. Did he suspect that she'd been less than genuine in accepting his invitation? Did it matter? she thought drily. She no longer had any intention of going out with him; it had been a foolish plan, formed in the heat of the moment. No—she would wait until she reached home and then tell him a firm goodbye...

She wasn't a complete fool. Leo was a devastatingly attractive male, wealthy and powerful, but she knew from experience how ruthless he could be.

'No response, Jacy? But then you always were a quiet girl, as I recall. It was one of the things I liked about you—that and your luscious body...' he drawled huskily.

Liar—he had never liked her at all. He'd made that abundantly clear when they'd parted, she thought, the old bitterness rising like gall in her throat. He had used her *luscious body* and he actually imagined that he was going to do the same again. As quickly as she'd dismissed the notion of revenge, angry pride had her reversing her decision. She would show him that the mature, adult Jacy Carter was more than a match for a lecherous snake like Leo Kozakis!

She recalled Liz's admonishment as she'd followed Jacy into the bedroom while she collected her coat to leave. 'Now don't blow it, Jacy. You only have to date him, not go to bed with him, and the Buddha is yours. But personally if I didn't have Tom I'd rather have Kozakis in my bed than a *netsuke* any day; the man positively smoulders.'

Jacy's lips twisted in a mockery of a smile. Liz was right about one thing: if she, Jacy, had *her* way, she would make damn sure that the man got burned. But how she was going to do it, she wasn't sure. She glanced out of the window, hoping for inspiration. They were driving along her street and in seconds she would be home. Gathering all her courage, she said, 'Stop here.'

The car slowed to a halt and she deliberately reached across the central console and laid a slender hand on Leo's thigh as he made to get out of the car. Jacy could feel the muscle tense beneath the fine fabric of his trousers, and she glanced up into his dark face to catch a flickering puzzlement in his brown eyes. 'You were mistaken, Leo. I had no objection to your driving me home, but I didn't want to drag you away from the party,' she explained throatily, amazed at her own acting ability. 'Promise me you will go back straight away, and I'll see you on Saturday at seven-thirty.' She had no intention of inviting him in for coffee, she wasn't yet confident enough; and, slowly gliding her hand from his thigh, she found the door-handle with her other hand. 'I live here—number twenty-seven—there's no need . . .'

'I'll see you to the door,' Leo cut in. 'And I *am* going back to Tom's. We still have business to discuss,' he offered with a quick smile.

Before she could get out, Leo, with a speed she wouldn't have thought him capable of, was around the front of the car and holding the passenger-door open for her.

He walked by her side up the stone steps that led to the entrance door of the small mews house that Jacy was lucky enough to own, thanks to an inheritance from her late father. She quickly delved into her handbag and found the door-key before raising her head and facing Leo. 'Thank you.'

'Till Saturday, Jacy.' His brown eyes, gleaming with satisfaction, captured hers. 'I'll be counting the hours.'

Before Jacy knew what was happening, his dark head bent and his lips brushed hers in the softest of kisses. Too surprised to resist, she made no comment as he deftly took the key from her hand, opened the door, and with one large hand in the middle of her back urged her inside. She turned and Leo pressed the key back into her hand.

'I won't come in now, but be ready, wanting and waiting for me on Saturday, sweetheart.'

Jacy shut the door with unnecessary force, the sound of his masculine laughter ringing in her ears and the image in her brain of his handsome, almost boyish, grin as he had turned to wave before leaping into his car. For a moment the years had rolled back and Leo had looked like the laughing, carefree fisherman she had first met in Corfu, and her heart had leapt in the same way as it had then. Angry with herself and furious with Leo Kozakis, Jacy strode across the hall and opened the door leading to her small living-room.

In the safety of her own private sanctum, she kicked off her shoes and shrugged out of her jacket, dropping it on to the arm of the large, soft-cushioned sofa before walking into her cosy kitchen. The familiar golden pine units, the bright blue gingham curtains at the small bay-window, and the row of flowering plants that she tended so carefully, all gave her a brief glow of satisfaction before she turned to the prettily tiled worktop and switched on the kettle. She needed a coffee, and to think... She rubbed her hands up over her eyes and into her hair, sighing as she did so. What had she let herself in for?

Five minutes later, with the coffee-cup in her hand, she returned to the living-room and sank into the comfortable sofa, curling her feet up beneath her. She slowly sipped the reviving brew then placed the empty cup on the low occasional-table in front of her. Her head dropped back against the large cushion and she closed her eyes.

Leo Kozakis, back in her life! Never in her worst nightmares had she expected to see the man again, and the adrenalin that had kept her reasonably in control for the past few hours suddenly deserted her.

Her golden eyes roamed around the room, her private haven. The muted green and rose of the Laura Ashley drapes at the window was continued in the loose covers of the sofa and two comfortable armchairs. The table between them, a lovingly polished mahogany, gleamed with a soft cinnamon hue that only years of loving care could develop. It had been in her mother's family for generations. She thought of her mother, killed in a car accident not long after the divorce, and for the first time in a decade wished she had a mother beside her to confide in.

A wry smile twisted Jacy's full lips; she had never confided in her mother at eighteen, and it was a bit late to regret it now. God, but it hurt! Seeing Leo tonight had brought it all back—the traumatic events of her nineteenth year. The pain, the disillusion, and the loneliness...

As a teenager Jacy had considered that she led a pretty normal, happy life. Her parents adored her and she lived in a nice house in Kent, not far from London. Her mother wrote children's books and her father was a journalist who, when she was thirteen, had taken an editor's job with a large American newspaper. Jacy had seen nothing unusual in her father's working in America and returning home several times a year: lots of her friends had fathers who worked abroad in the Middle East or in the Forces.

She and her mother had spent a couple of holidays in California, at the apartment that her father rented in Los Angeles; but the year Jacy completed her A levels it was decided she should have a year out before taking up her place at university where she intended reading politics, economics and philosophy. With two other girls she had travelled across Europe to Greece, and in the July they'd rented an apartment on the island of Corfu for a month. In that one month Jacy's life had changed completely; she had grown up with a vengeance...

A deep sigh tore from the depths of her heart. Jacy lifted her hand to her cheek and felt the dampness of cold tears. Jumping to her feet, she quickly walked out of the room and up the stairs to the bathroom. She hadn't cried in years and she wasn't about to start now, she told herself firmly. Stripping off her clothes, she turned on the shower and stepped beneath the warming spray.

But it was no good. Dried and dressed in pale blue silk pyjamas, she walked across the hall to her bedroom and crawled into bed, crushed by the weight of memories she had thought long forgotten. She tossed and turned for almost an hour, doing complicated maths in her head, deliberately recalling all the more difficult cases she had solved in her job, anything to try and block out the knowledge that Leo Kozakis had reappeared in her life.

Finally, as she listened to the clock on a nearby church peal out the stroke of two, she gave up and let her mind go back to the island of Corfu and her first meeting with Leo. Perhaps after so many years it would be a cleansing experience, she consoled herself. She could lay the unpleasant memories to rest once and for all, and go forward into the future with no baggage from the past to affect her life. For the first time, Jacy consciously admitted to herself that the affair with Leo Kozakis had coloured the way she saw all men.

Jacy sat on a smooth stone at the edge of the pebble beach, her golden eyes glued to the strange contraption fixed only about four feet from the water line. A large cage was resting in the shallow water; made of wire mesh but with a wood plank top, it was attached to the shore by a few strong ropes. But it was the contents that held her attention—struggling around inside the cage were about a dozen huge lobsters. Some fisherman's catch for the day, she knew, and she was torn between her undeniable liking for eating lobster and the idealism of a teenager that told her all living things should be free. A small chuckle escaped her; she could just imagine what would happen if she did free the poor lobsters! She would probably end up in a Greek jail...

A frown marred her smooth, lightly tanned brow. Would anyone care if she did? She was feeling rather sorry for herself and had been for the past two days. She had arrived at the apartment set on the hill above Paleokastritsa with her friends Joan and Anne a week ago, determined to have a month of rest and relaxation. Only it hadn't quite worked out like that.

It was very true—two was company and three a crowd, she thought ruefully. Joan and Anne had met a couple of young German tourists and decided to go with the young men on their very organised three-week walking and camping holiday around the whole island. Jacy couldn't help thinking that it was a very Teutonic trait to divide a beautiful island like Corfu into squares on a map and decide to camp in every one. It certainly wasn't Jacy's idea of a holiday; but then neither was being left on her own in a three-bedroom-apartment for the rest of the month.

She stretched out her long legs and dabbled her feet in the water, putting her hands behind her on the ground to support her lounging position. She was completely unaware of how stunning she looked. Her youthful face glowed with health and vitality, her long golden hair trailed over her shoulders in a mass of glittering curls, and the brief sea-green bikini she wore revealed every line of her curvaceous figure.

Paleokastritsa was perhaps the most beautiful place on Corfu, but today Jacy had walked from the tourist beach across the promontory to a small harbour, with the ferry-boats docked along one side and the glass-bottom boats that ran excursions from the harbour. A few fishing-boats also lay idly at anchor. Jacy had chosen the spot simply because the café only a few yards behind her was much less expensive than the ones around the main beach. She had just finished her lunch, a pizza and a glass of wine, and was wondering how she was going to spend the rest of the day when she'd spotted the lobster prison.

'With your colouring, you should be careful, lady—unless you want to end up looking like my lobsters.' A slightly accented voice broke into Jacy's reverie, and, straightening up, she turned her head to look at the man who had spoken.

She was struck dumb. She'd heard of Greek gods and seen pictures of the same, but the man standing to the left and slightly behind her was over six feet tall and breathtaking. Her eyes lifted up over a pair of long, muscular bronzed legs, parted as he straddled the sharp rocks at his feet. Skimpy denim cut-offs barely covered his essential maleness, and a line of black hair arrowed from beneath the denim over a hard flat belly to branch out over a broad chest in curling splendour. Wide shoulders supported a strong neck and proud head. Thick black curly hair tumbled over a wide brow and beautifully arched black eyebrows framed the deepest brown sparkling eyes Jacy had ever seen. A straight classic nose topped a generously curved mouth that widened in a brilliant smile.

'Your lobsters,' she murmured, and blushed scarlet at the sensual appreciation in his dark eyes. Thank God she hadn't set them free, she thought! He was obviously the fisherman, and she instantly hated the idea of upsetting the gorgeous man in any way.

'Yes, and perhaps I can persuade you to share one with me tonight.' He lowered his large frame down on to the ground beside her, seemingly impervious to the rocky terrain. 'That is if you don't already have a date?' he queried, his handsome face now much closer to her own.

'No—no, I don't,' she hastened to tell him, and found herself explaining her friends' desertion, unconsciously revealing the loneliness she had been feeling for the past two days.

'Friends like that you could do without,' he said shortly.

'Oh, I'm not blaming them,' she said hastily. She didn't want this lovely man to think she was a whingeing kind of girl. 'They...' She had been going to say 'fell in love', but somehow it seemed rather infantile, and not strictly true. She had slowly realised over the past few weeks that Joan and Anne were far more sophisticated and experienced than she herself was. They had dated quite a few men on their travels, sometimes staying away all night, and Jacy had begun to feel like a naïve child in comparison.

'They will have my undying gratitude, little girl, if you will just tell me your name and allow me to entertain you for the rest of your holiday.'

Jacy lifted her head and looked at the man now sitting beside her. 'It's Jacy,' she said shyly.

'Jacy—a lovely name for a lovely girl.' And, placing his large tanned hand over hers on the earth, he added, 'I am Leo.' He lifted her hand and without the support she fell sideways against him as he solemnly shook her hand.

The brush of her bare arm against his chest sent quivers tingling down her spine. She blushed hotly at the unfamiliar feeling that his touch aroused but, re-membering her manners, with a shy smile she murmured, 'How do you do?'

'So formal. I like that.' His brown eyes twinkled with laughter as he studied her flushed face. His gaze dropped to the gentle curves of her breasts exposed by the tiny green bikini top, then back to her scarlet face. 'And you blush so becomingly,' he teased, then jumping to his feet he dragged her up to stand beside him. 'I'm delighted to make your acquaintance, Jacy, and if you will permit I will show you my beautiful island. I will be your own personal tour guide, hmm?'

'Yes please,' she said breathlessly, completely bewitched by the glint in his dark eyes and the warm smile lighting his handsome face. 'But what about your work?' she asked, glancing down at the lobster cage.

'What do you know about my work?' he demanded.

Jacy looked up into his now unsmiling face, surprised at the sudden harshness in his tone. It hit her forcibly; the laughing young man suddenly looked older, more mature, and she wondered just how old he was. 'Well ... noth ... nothing,' she stammered. Perhaps he felt she was belittling his job as a simple fisherman? Hastily she reassured him, 'I think being a fisherman must be very hard work—I only meant, can you take time off whenever you like?' She watched as his harsh face relaxed once more into a friendly smile.

'Let *me* worry about that, Jacy.' And, once more catching her hand in his, he led her along the shore to the pier. 'Come and I'll show you my boat, and if you're very good I'll teach you how to fish ...'

For Jacy, the next two weeks turned into a dream. Leo's boat was her first surprise: a very modern motorboat fitted out with a galley and large comfortable cabin and shower-room; and on deck all the fittings for big-game fishing. Leo briefly explained that he sometimes took people out shark-fishing. She automatically thought he meant tourists; it was only much later that she realised her mistake.

Their first dinner-date was spent on board the boat, sitting on the deck sharing succulently cooked lobster with a simple salad and a bottle of wine. The night sky was a mass of glittering stars and the moon on the dark water a perfect back-drop for the romantic meal. When after midnight he drove her back to her apartment in a rather beaten-up jeep, he kissed her lightly on the lips and murmured a husky goodnight, promising to call for her early the next morning. In bed she had gone over every minute of the evening in her mind. She'd learned that he was twenty-nine, and had been born in Corfu. Later when she looked back she realised how clever he had been. That was about all she had ever found out about him.

They spent long hot days sailing, swimming, laughing and joking, sharing almost every meal; it was paradise to Jacy, and day by day her fascination with Leo grew until she finally admitted to herself that she was for the first time in her young life in love.

The sight of Leo standing on the bow of the boat dressed in brief black Spandex trunks ready to dive into the deep blue of the Ionian Sea was enough to stop the breath in her throat. He was so male, a glorious golden-brown god, and she couldn't believe her luck that he had chosen her from all the lovely girls staying around Paleokastritsa.

'Come on, lazybones, join me!' Leo shouted from the water.

Jacy needed no further urging and, running to the side of the boat, she dived into the welcoming depths. 'Race you to the shore,' she shouted, and set off at a fast crawl for the small beach some two hundred yards away. They had dropped anchor at a small cove that Leo assured her was inaccessible from the land and completely private.

Suddenly something hard fastened around her slender ankle and she felt herself pulled beneath the surface of the water. Two strong arms wrapped around her bikini-clad body and a firm mouth closed over hers. She clung to his broad shoulders, the water around them doing nothing to cool the searing heat inside her as the kiss went on and on. She wrapped her long legs around his and their limbs became entwined. Finally, they floated to the surface and, breaking the kiss, both gasped lung-fulls of fresh air.

Still clinging to her, Leo looked into her dazed golden eyes. 'God, but I want you, Jacy!' His feet found the sea-bed, but Jacy was still out of her depth—in more ways than one.

'And I want you,' she sighed, her small hands curving around his neck and ruffling the long dark curls plastered to his proud head by the warm water. He was everything she had ever wanted, she realised; nothing else in the world mattered to her as much as this man. For a second her golden eyes shadowed. Was it wise to be so obsessed with one person? But then Leo's lips once more found hers and all her doubts vanished.

'Open your mouth for me,' he husked against her lips, and willingly she complied. His tongue explored the moist dark cavern and she reciprocated in kind. Her heart pounded in her chest as Leo slipped one hand around her neck and removed the halter-top of her bikini before sliding to cup one perfectly formed breast in the palm of his hand. His thumb stroked lightly over the rosy nipple, and she gasped into his mouth as her breast hardened with his touch. Her head fell back as he trailed a row of soft kisses down her throat to the now pouting peak of her breast, then his mouth closed over the rigid tip and a small cry escaped her parted lips. Her slender legs gripped his muscular thighs even tighter and she heard him groan low in his throat as he reluctantly lifted his head from her breast.

She felt the heated pulse of his arousal hard against the most sensitive part of her; only two tiny fragments of cloth separated them from the completion they both ached for. The gentle lapping of the water around them did nothing to assuage the burning desire reflected in the black eyes that met her dazed golden ones.

'I don't think I can stand much more, Jacy,' Leo rasped, and began walking to the beach. He stopped a few feet from the shore and slid his hands down over her waist to her thighs, and gently eased her on to her own two feet before curving his large hands around her buttocks and pulling her firmly against his bulging thighs. 'If you want me to stop, it will have to be now, Jacy. Feel what you do to me,' he demanded harshly. 'No woman has ever affected me the way you do.'

'It's the same for me,' Jacy whispered; and it was true. She was standing in two feet of water, naked except for tiny briefs, but she felt no shame, no embarrassment: everything that had happened over the last few days, every touch, kiss and caress had led her to this moment. Her eyes, wide and worshipping, wandered in awe over his magnificent torso, the sun beating down on his golden skin, the black curling hair on his chest tipped with glittering pearls of water. She watched the heavy rise and fall of his broad chest, his rapid breathing, and knew hers was the same. She shivered as he lifted his hands and cupped her full breasts, his brown eyes glittering almost black as he feasted on her near naked form, and then she was swept up in his arms and carried the last few feet to the water-line.

Leo laid her down on the hard wet sand and she stretched out her arms to him in the age-old symbol of surrender. 'God, but you're beautiful,' he rasped as he lowered himself down beside her. In one deft movement he removed her bikini briefs so that she was lying naked before him.

The bright sun burning down from a clear blue sky dazzled her eyes for a second, then she gasped as Leo rolled on top of her, his arms supporting him either side of her shoulders. With one leg he nudged her thighs apart so he was cradled in the well of her hips. She gave a startled gasp as she realised he was also naked, but then his dark head swooped down, his mouth finding her willingly parted lips.

With hands, tongue and teeth he caressed and stroked every naked inch of her until she was a molten, quivering mass of need. She clutched his broad shoulders and her mouth found the strong column of his throat and bit lightly as her nails raked down his broad back. His long fingers stroked between her parted thighs, finding the soft damp curls and parting the tender flesh beneath. Her back arched in sudden convulsion as his seeking fingers found the most sensitive feminine heart of her, and she groaned aloud at the exquisite tension, the new fluttering sensations in her womb, the almost painful anticipation of something miraculous. Then Leo's mouth closed over the turgid peak of one breast and drew on the sensitive tip in rhythm with his wickedly stroking fingers. She writhed beneath him, crying, 'Please . . . please.'

'I can't wait,' Leo moaned against her swollen breast. 'Are you protected?'

'No, but . . .' She didn't care: she loved him . . .

A string of what could only have been curses erupted from his mouth in a furious tirade, and with appalling abruptness he leaped to his feet and dived back into the sea.

Jacy was too stunned to move; she lay on the beach where he had left her, a shivering mass of frustration. Slowly she became aware of her surroundings—the glaring sun, her completely naked state, the water lapping at her feet. Broad daylight! No man had ever touched her before and yet with Leo she had lost all modesty, all her inhibitions vanishing at his slightest touch.

She sat up. Leo was almost back at the boat, his strong arms scything through the water as though all the hounds of hell were after him. She groaned out loud. What a fool she was! Of course Leo would expect her to be protected. He was a sensitive, caring man and he would never take the chance of making a girl pregnant. She should be grateful for his restraint, but somehow all she felt was a burning frustration, and deep down a secret wish that he had been as carried away as herself. She would quite like to have Leo's child; in fact, she would love to. A little brown-eyed, black-haired boy. She smiled to herself—maybe some day. Getting to her feet, she picked up her bikini bottom and slipped it on before setting off at a steady crawl for the boat.

'Sorry, Jacy.' Leo's rather stern countenance stared down at her as she reached the small ladder at the stern. 'I had to leave, or else...' He held out a hand to her and she took it and scrambled back on board.

'Or else what...?' she said breathlessly. Still topless, she had no notion of how seductive she looked. Her high breasts, the nipples hard, stood out pertly; whether it was because of the water or lingering traces of arousal— it didn't make much difference to the man beside her.

'Not what, where,' Leo growled, and, swinging her into his arms once more, he strode across the deck and down into the cabin, dropping Jacy on to the bunk from quite a height.

Laughing up at him, she met his eyes with hers and the laughter died in her throat. His handsome face was stern, almost angry. He had wrapped a towel around his waist, but that was all he wore. 'What's the matter?' she asked uncertainly; she had never seen him look so serious.

'Nothing's the matter now!' he said oddly. 'Hell, even swimming two hundred yards can't cure it,' he muttered, almost to himself, before joining her on the bunk.

'Do you think this is wise?' she managed to ask before once again his lips met hers in a long drugging kiss. Within seconds the passion that had flared on the beach was once more ignited and Jacy cried out as with lips and hands he once more aroused her to fever pitch: but this time there was no stopping.

Leo lifted his head from teasing her swollen breasts, and holding out a small foil package he murmured, 'Put it on for me, Jacy.'

For a second she didn't know what he was asking, and when she did she still trembled. Her hot, curious gaze slid down between their two bodies, the evidence of his manhood intimidating. 'I . . .' She tentatively stroked her slender hand over his hard flat stomach. How could she tell him that she'd never seen a naked man before? Never made love? Explain her virginal fear? How could she explain all this when her body reacted with wanton delight to his every touch?

'You're shy,' he groaned, 'and I can't hold out.'

Then once more their lips met and Leo slid his hands beneath her buttocks and lifted her up to him. Jacy tensed for a split-second, felt one last lingering flash of fear at what was about to happen, and then he was inside her. She flinched at the swift stab of pain, and Leo stilled.

'Jacy, why didn't you say?' he rasped, his dark eyes black with passion burning down into hers.

'Please don't stop,' she pleaded, all her love and longing there for him to see in her huge eyes, and with a muffled groan he buried his head in her throat and began to move slowly and firmly.

'I love you, I love you, Leo,' she heard herself scream as her slender body convulsed in a mind-bending explosion of rapture; and she only vaguely heard Leo's equally exultant cry as with one last thrust his great body shuddered out of his control before he collapsed on top of her.

For a long lingering moment the only sound was of their heavy breathing mingled with the gentle lapping of the water against the hull of the boat. Jacy had never felt so happy, so contented, so sated in her whole life. Leo's sweat-slicked body covered hers like a great loving

security-blanket. He was hers for all time, she thought
delightedly.

'My first virgin,' he breathed raggedly against her
throat, and as he lifted his head his dark eyes, still dilated with passion, studied her softly flushed face. 'But
you should have told me, Jacy. I would have been more
gentle. Are you all right?'

'All right? No,' she murmured, and thrilled at the
quick flash of concern in his eyes. 'I'm ecstatic, in
heaven, in love. I never knew anything could be so won-
derful,' she freely confessed, before asking, 'Is it always
like this?'

'Between you and me, I have a suspicion it will always
be perfect.'

'Just a suspicion?' she teased, confident in her new-
found love.

Leo's head lowered and he breathed against her lips.
'God help me, it's a certainty.'

CHAPTER THREE

JACY SANG as she rushed around the small apartment making sure everything was perfect for the intimate dinner for two she had planned. A quick look in the oven . . . yes, the fillet of lamb was almost cooked to perfection. Straightening, she glanced out of the window; it was already dark but even at night the view was spectacular. The apartment was one of a block of four perched halfway up the hill-side above the bay of Paleokastritsa, and the twinkling lights below, the moon on the water, all added to her sense of wonder at the paradise she had found herself in—and the man who had made it all perfect . . .

Leo would be arriving any minute, she thought happily as she walked back into the living-room. It was a simple room: white-washed walls and one or two pictures of the island added for a bit of colour. A large, comfortable sofa-bed, a couple of chairs and a coffee-table—the minimum of furniture needed to equip an apartment to be rented to tourists, but still she loved it.

The past three days had been magical; from the afternoon on Leo's boat when he had made her his, she had been living in a rosy glow of love. A soft, reminiscent smile curved her full lips. It had been night by the time they'd finally upped anchor and made for the harbour, after spending hours making love. Leo was everything she had ever dreamed of. A tender, sensitive lover and an expert teacher.

By the time they had finally reached the harbour, Jacy, confident in his love, had jumped from the boat and following his instructions had helped him tie it up. Unthinkingly she remarked, 'I think I will make a great fisherman's wife,' and his laughing reply, 'I'm sure you will, Jacy,' had only confirmed her happiness.

Jacy frowned slightly; the only cloud on her horizon was her mother. She had rung England earlier today and spoken to her. There were only four days of her holiday left, and it had seemed only fair to tell her mother that the chances were she would not be returning home, or going to university in September—because of Leo. Unfortunately, her mother's reaction had not been enthusiastic. She had responded by telling Jacy that her father was at present in England, and she'd better get home and discuss the future with both of them before doing anything rash. Jacy hadn't quite had the nerve to confess that she was already committed body and soul to her Greek fisherman.

The banging of a car door wiped the frown from her forehead, and with a leap of her pulse she dashed to open the door. 'Leo.' She said his name, her eyes drinking in the sight of his tall, hard body that was dressed casually in cream pleated trousers and a cream polo-shirt. He lounged elegantly against the door-frame, and in one hand he carried a bottle of champagne, in the other a bunch of gorgeous yellow roses.

'Golden flowers for a golden girl.' Leo smiled down at her, then, bending his head, he brushed his lips lightly across hers.

Her breath caught in her throat. He was so handsome and somehow different from the laughing fisherman she had fallen in love with: more mature, sophisticated. If she hadn't known better she could have quite easily mistaken him for a debonair man-about-town. She shook her head, her long golden hair shimmering in the half-light. She was being fanciful; it *was* her Leo, and tonight she was sure would be a milestone in their relationship.

Her feminine intuition was working overtime: surely tonight he would formally propose? She took the flowers he offered and, suddenly inexplicably shy, buried her face in the sweet-scented blooms.

'Thank you, they're beautiful,' she murmured huskily.

Putting his arm around her shoulders, Leo chuckled. 'Be careful, sweetheart. Don't forget the thorns. I would hate to see your lovely face spoilt.'

Lifting her head, she beamed up at him. 'So you only love me for my looks?' she teased. In the security of his embrace, she felt the most treasured, the most loved girl alive.

'Well, maybe not just your looks—your body has an awful lot to do with it,' he drawled with a lascivious grin.

Their joined laughter set the tone for the evening. They ate in the kitchen, by candlelight; two lovers in a world of their own, joking and laughing in between eating the typically English meal that she'd prepared: roast lamb, mint-sauce, and roast potatoes with Yorkshire pudding plus a selection of vegetables.

'What are you trying to do to me?' Leo groaned, a lazy smile twitching the corners of his sensuous mouth as he laid down his spoon, having finished the final scrap of cold summer-pudding. 'Get at my heart through my stomach?'

She grinned back. 'Would you mind?'

'No.' He looked surprised. 'No, I don't think I would.' He was silent for a moment, his dark eyes narrowed assessingly on her young face before, with an impatient gesture, he pushed back his chair and jumped up. 'Come on, let's finish this bottle in the living-room.'

Jacy had an uneasy feeling that something had upset him, so she meekly picked up the two glasses and followed him through into the other room. But she quickly dismissed her fears as Leo, reclining on the sofa with his long legs stretched out in front of him, beckoned her into his waiting arms. She placed the glasses on the coffee-table and curled up beside him, welcoming the warmth of his arm around her naked shoulders. Tonight she had worn the only dress that she had with her: a slim blue fine jersey sheath that tied with a draw-string between her breasts—more a beach dress than anything else, but when one's only luggage was a haversack there was no room for fancy clothes.

'You're quiet, sweetheart—something wrong?' Leo murmured, nuzzling her ear.

'No,' she sighed. 'I was just wishing I had a wardrobe of beautiful clothes to beguile you with.' She chuckled, lazily running her small hand over his broad chest. 'All you've seen me in so far is a bikini, or shorts and trousers, and...'

'My darling girl——' his mouth slid down over the soft curve of her neck, and lower '—I don't care *what* you wear—in fact I prefer you naked any time.' His teeth pulled at the draw-string bow between the soft curves of her breasts.

Jacy looked down at his dark head resting on her breast and, lifting her hand, stroked her fingers through the thick black curling hair of his head, delighting in the silky feel, the subtle scent of him, all male...and all hers. 'Time is another problem,' she murmured faintly.

Leo raised his head. 'A problem?'

'Yes.' And, taking her courage in both hands, she told him, 'The girls will be back any day now, and my ticket back to England is for Friday, in three days' time.' The thought of leaving Corfu and Leo terrified her. 'I don't want to leave you,' she blurted. With one slender finger she traced the outline of his eyebrow, the strong line of his nose, and around the generous curve of his mouth that could delight her in ways she had never thought possible. She loved him with all her heart, mind and body, and, leaning forward, she pressed her mouth to his, her tongue darting between his strong teeth. She wanted him; God, how she wanted him...

Leo allowed her to take the initiative for a moment before folding her tight in his arms, his tongue meeting and moving with hers as the kiss deepened into a flaring of passion so intense that liquid heat flooded Jacy's body and she burned with need. Her hands curved around his neck, her fingers tangling in the night-black hair of his head while Leo lifted her legs across his lap and laid her back against the sofa.

'Don't go, then,' he muttered thickly as he broke the kiss, his strong hand stroking down over her breast, taking the bodice of her dress with it. 'Stay here with me.' His fingers found her tender nipple and rolled it between thumb and forefinger. His brown eyes, gleaming with growing desire, captured hers. 'You want to. You want me,' he said hardly. 'You know you do.'

His hand at her breast, the darkening glitter in his eyes, and the heat of his hard body against her promised everything. It was what she had been longing to hear. He wanted to marry her.

'Oh, yes, Leo. Yes. I want to spend my life with you.' She felt the tremor through his huge body at her words; his hand fell from her breast and, as if in slow motion, he leant back to stare down at her flushed, beautiful face.

'You're very young, Jacy—your whole life is a long time,' he said, with an odd inflection in his throaty voice.

Guilelessly she traced her small hands up over his hard biceps to his shoulders. 'Not long enough for the way I feel about you, Leo.' At last, after two weeks of waiting, they were finally making a commitment, she thought ecstatically. Leo loved her, he wanted her to stay; her dream had come true. She slid her hands from his shoulders to cup his beloved face in her small palms. 'Kiss me,' she demanded, wanting to seal their future. But before his lips met hers a loud knock on the door interrupted their idyll.

'Are you expecting someone?' Leo demanded, drawing away from her.

Hastily she scrambled off his lap and adjusted her dress. 'No, no one—unless the girls have come back early.' The banging on the door continued. So much for her romantic evening, she thought sadly and with some frustration.

'You'd better answer it,' Leo commanded, leaning forward to pick up his glass of wine from the table. 'And get rid of them, if you can.' He glanced up at her flushed, woeful expression and grinned. 'If you can't, we could go night-fishing!'

Relieved that their evening wasn't to end so precipitately, she grinned back before heading for the door and opening it.

'What took you so long?' a hard male voice demanded.

'Daddy! What are you doing here?' she got out, before being swept off her feet in a bear-hug and carried back into the living-room.

'I came to see you, Ja...' She was dropped to her feet so abruptly that she nearly fell as her father caught sight of Leo. 'My God! Kozakis!' he exclaimed, completely ignoring his daughter.

Jacy stirred restlessly in the bed. Ten years on and the memory was still painful. She could see the whole scene in her mind's eye as if it were yesterday, the players moving seemingly in slow motion.

The small room, and her father, a tall slim man with fair hair, about the same height as Leo but a good deal older. He stood motionless, a questioning light in his pale eyes.

But Leo jumped to his feet, overturning in the process the small occasional-table that held the wine and glasses.

'What the hell are you doing here, Carter? Hoping to get a follow-up for your filthy rag?' he snarled, and in two short strides he was standing within inches of the other man and grasping him by the throat. 'Get out before I break your damn neck.'

'No, no!' Jacy didn't know what was happening, but there was no mistaking the burning hatred in Leo's eyes. 'Please, Leo, this is my father,' she cried.

Leo's hands fell to his sides and he turned slowly to face Jacy. For a moment he watched her in a bitter, hostile silence. 'This man is your *father*? You *knew*. You knew all the time who I was.'

She flinched at the icy contempt in his tone, and couldn't speak: fear had closed her throat. The dark man towering over her, who only minutes earlier had been making love to her, had vanished, and in his place stood a stranger. A steely-eyed, furious stranger.

'I suppose you're following in your father's footsteps as a budding reporter?' he queried with deadly softness.

'I thought about it,' she responded meekly, hoping to defuse the violent tension in the room. But...

'I should have guessed all that dewy-eyed innocence was too good to be true. What was it to be? A scoop to launch your career? How Kozakis seduced an innocent girl?' His lips curled in sneering contempt, his dark eyes narrowed to mere slits. 'Just you try it, Jacy—you *or* your father—and I will make you out to be the biggest slut in Christendom.'

Jacy, her legs trembling and her eyes filling with moisture, fought back her tears. She didn't know what had gone wrong. She could not understand what was happening—why Leo, her lover, was behaving this way. And she was too terrified to ask.

'Or perhaps you were going for the biggy, a wedding-ring, then the fat settlement and an exposé. My God! I nearly fell for it.'

She heard Leo's ranting, and her rosy dream of love and marriage to her fisherman disintegrated before her eyes. Her glance swung to her father, and she was hurt anew by the look of stunned disbelief on her father's face.

'Now, wait a damn minute, Kozakis. You can't speak to my daughter like that.' Her father finally found his voice; but as Jacy watched Leo pushed past the older man and strode towards the door. With his hand on the door-handle, he turned and spoke.

'Carter, I always knew you were a slimy rat.' His dark, furious gaze slanted between father and daughter. 'And the old adage is certainly true: like father, like daughter.' His black eyes caught and held Jacy's. 'At least a whore has the basic honesty to state a price, but women like you turn my stomach. Your type bleed a man dry before the poor sod even knows he's paying for it.' And with one disgusted shake of his dark head he stormed out of the apartment, slamming the door after him.

Jacy gave one despairing little cry. 'Leo...' But in her heart she knew it was too late. She staggered to the sofa and collapsed on to it in a heap. Burying her head in her hands, she cried and cried as her heart splintered into a million pieces. She was barely aware of the comforting arm of her father around her shaking shoulders. She didn't fully understand what had happened, but Leo's parting words had cut into her very soul. The icy contempt in his dark eyes was indelibly burnt into her brain.

'Hush, Jacy, please. The man's not worth it.' Her father's quietly voiced words finally penetrated the black depths of her sorrow.

'But I love him,' she rasped, her throat dry with crying. 'I don't understand . . .' she wailed and, lifting her head, with her eyes swollen and red with weeping, she beseeched her father, 'What happened? We love each other,' she ended on a sob.

'I don't know what has been going on here, Jacy; your mother gave me some garbled story about your wanting to marry a fisherman.'

'Yes, Daddy—Leo. But . . .'

'Sorry, my pet.' He held her close, an arm around her shoulder. 'But Leo Kozakis is no fisherman. He's a very wealthy businessman, with offices in all the major capitals of the world. Whatever he told you was a lie: his family home is a luxurious villa not far from here, and it's guarded like Fort Knox.'

As her father spoke Jacy felt the full weight of Leo's betrayal sink deeper and deeper into every fibre of her being. She felt sick and, worse, utterly humiliated and ashamed. She had given her most precious gift to a liar and a cheat. 'Are you sure he's the same man?' She made one last appeal, hoping there might be some mistake.

'Jacy, I'm sure,' he confirmed soberly. 'But if he's hurt you in any way, I'll make him pay—even if I have to follow him for the rest of my days.'

She looked into her father's familiar face and was shocked by the grim determination in his usually easygoing features. His pale eyes gleamed as cold as the Arctic Ocean. 'If that man has seduced you, my baby . . .'

'No, Daddy.' She stopped him. 'It didn't go that far,' she lied. Even in her distress she recognised that there was no way a man like her father would ever win a fight against Leo.

Suddenly, all the little things that she'd puzzled over in the past few weeks made complete sense. The luxurious boat—of course he didn't take out tourists; he probably enjoyed game fishing . . . The lobsters she'd seen on the

very first day they'd met—obviously he had *bought* the
catch. The amount of free time Leo had spent with her;
no fisherman could afford that kind of leisure.

She groaned inwardly at her own naïve folly. The *look*
of the man alone should have told her. Tonight, when
he'd arrived at her door elegantly dressed, she had wondered for a moment how a Greek fisherman could afford
that kind of attire. But perhaps most telling of all was
his complete grasp of the English language, with hardly
a trace of accent. She had once queried it, and Leo had
laughingly said he'd picked it up from English friends.

'You're sure, Jacy? I know the man's reputation.'

'Positive,' she declared, and was amazed to hear how
emphatic she sounded when it was taking every ounce
of control she possessed to stop herself from screaming
hysterically at the fate that had dealt her such a devastating blow. But somewhere in her subconscious she
recognised the ruthless power of a man like Leo, and
instinctively she knew that he was the type to crush her
father without a second thought, if it suited him.

Exactly *how* she knew, she could not analyse. Her
chaotic emotions weren't conducive to clear thinking.
All she *did* recognise as she stood curved in her father's
arm, was that the man she loved did not exist, and all
she had left to cling to was her father. Later she would
question every word, every gesture in bitter self-
recrimination; but at the moment she just wanted some
explanation, some excuse for the pain she was feeling.
She recalled her father's face as he'd walked in the door
and spotted Leo.

'But how do *you* know Leo, Daddy?' she asked, unconscious of the pained puzzlement in her delicately expressive features.

'Oh, baby, it's a long story, and not very pleasant.'

'Please, Daddy, I need to know, to understand.'

'I guess I owe you that much, Jacy.' A deep frown marked his even features, the lines around his pale eyes exaggerated as he stared down into the trusting, up-turned face of his daughter. 'It's not a pleasant story, child.' Taking a deep breath, he continued speaking in an even tone, showing little emotion. 'You know the paper I edit in Los Angeles? Well, a few months back Leo Kozakis was the headline story for quite some time. The lady he'd lived with for three years in San Francisco was suing him for palimony.'

Jacy's face went even paler, if that was possible, at the mention of another woman. 'Palimony?' She had never heard the word.

'Yes, Jacy; in California, a man doesn't have to be married to a woman to be sued for alimony—it's enough if they've lived together for a few years as man and wife. In Leo Kozakis' case, the woman claimed that she'd lived with him for three years in his penthouse apartment, and then he'd thrown her out. She applied to the court for palimony, and Kozakis fought the case. His ar-gument was that the lady was his mistress, nothing more, and that she'd clearly understood the situation before she moved into the apartment.'

'That's disgusting,' Jacy murmured.

'Yes, well, Kozakis reckoned that it was a common arrangement in Europe. He gave the lady presents when he saw her, and when she declared that she was homeless he allowed her to use the company apartment. But at no time had he made any commitment to her. It was a very nasty fight.'

Jacy could not bear to believe it. It was something so outside of her teenage idea of love and life. To fight in a Court of law, not even over a marriage but simply over one's *love-life*, was too horrible to contemplate. 'What happened?' she whispered.

'Kozakis won, of course. Unfortunately for you, my pet. It was my paper, my decision to break the story to the public, and we tended towards the lady's side of the problem. Kozakis knows that, and he's never forgiven me. Obviously when I walked in here tonight, and you told him that I was your father, he must have thought it was a set-up—you and I working together on another exposé of his lifestyle.'

'Oh God! So *that's* why he asked if I was going to be a reporter!' Jacy spoke her thoughts out loud. The worst thing was that she'd confirmed Leo's suspicions by agreeing that she *had* considered a career in journalism. He'd cut her off before she could add that she wasn't going to.

'I'm sorry, truly sorry, if I've ruined your budding romance, but as your father I've got to tell you that the man would never have married you. His type never do: he just enjoys beautiful women.'

Each word her father spoke was like a knife in Jacy's heart, but she didn't doubt for a moment that he was telling her the truth.

'He's known to have girlfriends dotted all over the world, wherever the firm of Kozakis does business. I had heard that his father is ill, which is probably why Leo is here at the family home in Corfu. I hate to see you disillusioned, child——' his hand gently stroked over her golden hair in a consoling gesture '—but I imagine that he found a young girl like you nothing more than a novel diversion while he has to stay here in Corfu.'

A blessed numbness had enveloped Jacy as she listened to the horrible truth, and she knew that her father was right. Almost dispassionately she recalled the first time Leo had made love to her, and a bitter, ironic smile twisted her full lips. He had almost taken her on the beach, but he'd been nowhere near as out of control as she herself had been. She understood clearly now why, when she'd admitted to being unprotected, he had quite cold-bloodedly left her and swum back to the boat. Later, when he was adequately protected, only then had he made love to her. While she'd been dreaming of wedding-bells and little brown-eyed babies, he'd been making quite sure that he wouldn't be compromised into a hasty marriage.

'You've had a lucky escape, Jacy. At least the man had the decency not to seduce you completely. You're young, and it's your first crush on an older man. I know it hurts, but believe me, child, you'll soon get over it. Once you get home and go to university, all this will seem like a brief holiday romance that didn't come to anything.'

Jacy turned over on her stomach and buried her head in the pillow. Her father had been right, in a way. They had left Corfu together the next day, and she'd gone on to university; but she had never been the same carefree young girl again. That summer in Corfu she had grown up... Then in the autumn, her parents had told her that they were getting a divorce—apparently they'd only stayed together until she left home.

It had been another blow to her, and she had seen little of her father over the next few years. Then when her mother was so tragically killed he had returned to London and bought this house, and Jacy had shared it with him until his death.

With hindsight, she could see why her faith in men and marriage was non-existent, but for a long time she'd been terribly hurt by what she saw as betrayal by the only men she had ever known. Her student years were spent studying hard and taking little part in the social side of college—and avoiding men like the plague. She obtained a First in Economics, and joined Mutual as an executive; and until tonight she'd been completely happy with her career and lifestyle.

Yawning widely, she snuggled down into the depths of her single bed. So Leo Kozakis had reappeared in her life! She would not allow him to ruin her happiness again. She was a mature, successful woman, not the silly girl he had known. She could handle him, she told herself as her eyelids drooped. In fact, it would be a pleasure to teach the arrogant devil that he couldn't have every woman he desired. She had read articles about him over the years, and it appeared to her that he'd never changed at all: he was still the womanising rake he'd always been, whereas Jacy considered that *she* had grown into a strong, capable woman—a match for any male chauvinist pig of the Kozakis type. And on that thought she finally drifted into sleep.

Jacy was naked on a beach. The sea, a raging grey torrent, lashed the shore-line, barely missing her feet as she ran along the hard sand as though her heart would burst. A terrified glance over her shoulder showed her that he was still in pursuit—a large, dark, faceless man. Her lungs expanded in raw agony with every step she took. He was gaining on her. She felt hot breath and the hairs on the back of her neck stood upright in terror; harsh breathing mingled with her own rasping breath, and then in the distance a bell rang, getting louder by the second. She gasped and struggled violently.

Opening her eyes, Jacy groaned out loud. She was lying upside-down in the bed, the sheet twisted like a strait-jacket around her and her slender body damp with perspiration. Battling her way out of the tangled mess of covers, she swung her long legs over the side of the bed and, brushing the long mane of her hair from her face, she reached for the jangling phone on the bedside-table. God! That was some nightmare, she thought with a shiver as she lifted the receiver to her ear.

'Hello, Jacy here.' It was Liz's cheerful voice at the other end. 'What time of the morning do you call this?' Jacy demanded, casting a glance at the clock beside the telephone.

'Seven—but I wanted to catch you before you left for work. How did it go last night with Leo? Did he make a pass at you?'

'Please, Liz, one question at a time,' she groaned, rubbing the sleep from her eyes with one hand. 'It went fine. He brought me home and said goodnight at the door and, no, he didn't kiss me.' Thank God Liz couldn't see her fingers crossed behind her back.

'Well, that's something, I suppose. Listen, Jacy, I don't think it's a good idea for you to date Kozakis. We'll just forget about the bet, hmm?'

Jacy straightened, suddenly aware of the unease in her friend's voice. 'And what's brought about this change of heart? Frightened you might lose the *netsuke*? As I remember, last night you were doing your damnedest to fix me up with Mr Kozakis,' she drawled mockingly. Liz was up to something...

'Yes, I know, but I only have your best interests at heart. I'd only met Leo once before, and I found him charming. Well, let's face it—the man *is* charming! But I had a talk to Tom last night, and he told me that Kozakis is a brilliant businessman, but where women are concerned, he's strictly the love 'em and leave 'em type. You're much too naïve to get mixed up with a man like that.'

'Naïve?' Jacy snorted. 'Hardly, Liz.'

'You know what I mean. You might be good in business, but your relationships with men are virtually non-existent. I don't know how you knew Leo Kozakis before, or what happened—you can tell me some time—but I don't think he's the right sort of man for you.'

'Is there something you're not telling me?' Jacy queried. Liz's mission in life for years had been to fix her up with a man, and now, in a complete turnabout, she was trying to do the opposite.

'All right, I'll come clean. Leo Kozakis returned to the party last night. Now, I know he's supposed to be taking you out to dinner on Saturday, and yet quite brazenly in front of me he offered to take Thelma home. The cheek of the man!' Her indignation echoed 'own the telephone.

Jacy burst out laughing, but there was very little humour in it. Thelma was the tall blonde she had seen Leo dancing with earlier last night. The man was certainly running true to form. 'Oh, Liz, I would love to have seen your face.'

'It wasn't funny. Thelma might be a great interior designer, but her reputation for trying out all the beds she instals is well-known. That isn't the sort of date I had in mind when I made the bet with you.'

'Sorry, Liz, the bet still stands,' Jacy heard herself saying firmly. 'Look at it from my point of view. I get wined and dined for free, and win the *netsuke*, while the great man gets nothing from me in return except my company. His baser instincts he can indulge with the lovely Thelma.'

'That's a dangerous game to play—Kozakis is a devious man. I wasn't going to say anything, but Tom admitted last night that he'd known all about the party for a week—the boys had told him. He said nothing so as not to upset me, but, apparently, when he mentioned it to Kozakis the man insisted on coming back with him last night for some papers that weren't all that important, after enquiring if you would be attending. He'd seen a snapshot of you at our place in Surrey last week. Tom thinks the man is hunting you down,' Liz warned.

'But I suppose you know what you're doing. At least, I hope you do...'

Jacy sat for some minutes after replacing the telephone, going over the conversation in her head. So Leo had known she was going to be there last night. But why bother after all this time? She frowned... But of course, the explanation was simple and so true to form... Leo was in London for the first time in ages—how much quicker it was to take up with an old flame, a meal and then straight to bed, than to have to find a new woman and waste time building a relationship.

She smiled. It was a good feeling to know that Liz cared about her well-being. But the information about Leo and his involvement with Thelma was the one thing designed to strengthen her determination. Leo Kozakis would get a taste of his own medicine for a change, she vowed.

Later that morning, when she walked into the foyer of the Mutual Save and Trust Company and saw Barbara at the reception desk, the young girl's face puffy and her eyes red-rimmed from crying, all her previous anger resurrected. Jacy had suffered like that herself at Leo Kozakis' hands. She'd never considered herself to be a vengeful person, but a burning desire to get even with Leo for herself and all her sisters who'd suffered at the hands of such men consumed her usually logical mind. Confidently, she told herself that this time she would turn the tables on the conceited swine. She was looking forward to Saturday night...

CHAPTER FOUR

JACY wasn't a conceited girl, but the reflection that stared back at her from the mirrored-door of her wardrobe brought a self-satisfied smile to her wide mouth. She had swept her long blonde hair into an intricate twist on top of her head and fastened it with a black and gold antique clip. She had taken time with her make-up, using slightly more than usual, and the taupe eyeshadow skilfully blended with a touch of dark gold emphasised the strange yellow glint of her wide eyes. A brown mascara elongated her already long lashes, the whole outlined with the faintest touch of brown kohl. The addition of blusher to her foundation highlighted her classic cheekbones, and the subtle plum-coloured lipstick outlined her full mouth in a sensuous curve.

She turned sideways and back, the better to admire her ensemble. The extravagantly rainbow-coloured, beaded swing-jacket moved subtly as she turned, and the matching black bustier, with identical colourful beading tracing the curve of her full breasts, fitted to perfection. It was a Diane Freis design, purchased that very afternoon from the designer room on the first floor at Harrods, and, yes—it had been a good buy. She'd teamed the jacket and bustier with her favourite black silk, short evening skirt that clung lovingly to her slim hips and ended just above her knee. Her stockings were a muted barely black, and her shoes were soft black leather mules with a bobbin-shaped inch-and-a-half heel. The overall effect was stunning.

After spending all morning going through her
wardrobe, she had finally decided to treat herself to
something new. She didn't question the reason behind
it, telling herself that it was a justifiable purchase. Yet
she had a very good wardrobe. A selection of classic
suits for work, plus a good range of casual gear. Calvin
Klein figured largely in her wardrobe: she loved the
American designer's easy, elegant style. She also adored
his perfume, Obsession, and, picking up a bottle from
the dresser, she liberally sprayed the long curve of her
neck. Finally she fitted a pair of black and glass beaded
cascade earrings to her ears, and she was ready. The
epitome of sophisticated womanhood, she told herself
with a grin.

She was lucky in one respect, she supposed. As a single
girl living in London she didn't have the expense of
buying or renting an apartment, having inherited her
father's mews cottage and also a fairly decent amount
of insurance money on his death. She wasn't wealthy,
she would always have to work, but she did have a very
nice nest-egg that allowed her to indulge herself
occasionally.

A knock followed by the ringing of the doorbell made
her stiffen imperceptibly; but with a last look around
the bedroom she picked up a small clutch handbag and
hastily made her way downstairs to the front door.
Taking a deep breath, she opened it.

All the mature confidence in the world couldn't
prevent her mouth falling open in stunned shock at the
sight that met her eyes. Leo stood negligently against the
door-frame, immaculately dressed in a formal evening
suit, a pristine white dress-shirt with an elegantly tied
bow-tie in deepest navy settled at his strong throat.
Across his broad shoulders was casually draped a long,
navy cashmere overcoat; but it was his face and hands
that caused her stunned immobility. His dark eyes

gleamed with a secret knowledge and his sensuous lips were parted in a wide smile as his large hands held out towards her a bunch of yellow roses and a bottle of champagne...

'Golden flowers for a golden girl.' He pressed the roses into her cold hand.

Mechanically she took them, muttering, 'Thank you. I'll just put them in water.' And turning she fled through the living-room and into the kitchen. How dared he remind her of their last date all those years ago? she fumed. Either he was the most insensitive clod on God's earth or he had done it deliberately to discover her reaction; and she had a sinking feeling that the second premise was correct.

Standing in the kitchen, she took a few deep breaths before opening a wall cupboard and removing a large pottery vase, the first one she touched. Filling it with water, she stuffed the offending roses in the container.

'That's no way to treat such delicate flowers.' Leo's breath moved the short hairs on the back of her neck. He had followed her into the kitchen.

Jacy spun around. He was much too close, his tall presence was overpowering in the small room. 'Yes, well—I can arrange them later. I thought we were going out to dinner. I'm starving.' She was babbling, she knew, but suddenly it hit her. Her crazy idea to teach this man a lesson was just that: crazy.

'Oh, I think we have time for a drink, Jacy. A glass of champagne, a toast to old friends, hmm?'

'A little less of the old,' she drawled mockingly. 'And I never drink on an empty stomach.' Bravely facing him, while trying desperately to regain her shattered nerves, she added, 'Shall we go?' She just wanted to get the evening over with as quickly as possible, and then she would never see Leo Kozakis again. His deeply tanned face and the overt sexual gleam in his seductive brown

eyes threatened her in ways she had thought long
forgotten.

An unfathomable expression flitted across his
handsome features, and she wondered for a second if he
would be quite so easy to get rid of. She should never
have agreed to see him, she realised, when to her astonishment she found herself crushed against his hard body.

Her head fell back against his arm, and her lips parted
to object when his mouth swooped down on hers, taking
full advantage of her half-open mouth. Her bag fell to
the floor as she clutched at his upper arms in an effort
to restrain him, but his tongue darted provocatively into
her mouth in an achingly familiar kiss. She tried to
remain frozen in his hold, but as his shockingly sensual
mouth ravaged hers she could feel the fierce curl of
longing knot in her stomach.

She was going mad. She hated the man, but then as
his hands moved lower and slid beneath her jacket,
hauling her slender body tightly against his hard frame
and flattening her breasts against his broad muscular
chest, she trembled. But Leo wasn't immune either; she
felt the shudder that ran through him and the sudden
hardening of his thighs before, with a rasping groan, he
pushed her slightly away from him, breaking the kiss.
She was mortified at the ease with which he had evoked
her response and a red tide of colour suffused her throat
and face.

'How dare you?' she blurted like some Regency virgin.

'I always think it is best to get the first kiss out of the
way early, otherwise it can quite spoil one's dinner wondering if the chemistry is there,' he opined mockingly
and then, retrieving her bag from the floor, he held it
out to her.

She took it without a word, too furious to speak. But
Leo had no such problem.

'You're looking beautiful, Jacy, and I could happily stay here all night.' He ran a comprehensive eye over her, then smiled suggestively. 'But you were right, I find I am rather hungry myself. The champagne can keep until we return.'

To Jacy's stupefaction, acting as though he owned the place, he opened the refrigerator door and placed the bottle inside before turning to catch hold of her elbow and lead her out of her own house. She was seated in the front seat of his car, her seat-belt fastened securely over her body by an attentive Leo, before she could regain some control over her wildly fluctuating emotions. She wanted to scream at him for his high-handed treatment of her, but common sense prevailed and, with a degree of civility, she managed to ask conversationally, 'Where are you taking me to dine?' She cast a sidelong glance at her companion.

His handsome profile looked carved out of granite, and as she watched the firmly chiselled mouth tightened imperceptibly, almost as if he were reluctant to answer her simple question. Finally he turned slightly towards her, taking his eyes from the road for an instant. 'I hope you don't mind, but I have to attend a private dinner-dance at the Ritz; a cousin's twenty-first.'

'A private party?' she repeated. That wasn't what she had expected. A quiet dinner for two in some fashionable restaurant was Leo Kozakis' style, but certainly not an introduction to the Kozakis clan. 'But...'

'I know it is not what you expected——' Leo cut off her objection before she could voice it, his attention once more on the road ahead '—but we needn't stay long, and later I will take you somewhere more intimate, if you like,' he drawled provocatively.

Jacy said nothing, ignoring the challenge in his statement. But she couldn't help but recognise the irony

of the situation. Years ago she would have been delighted to meet Leo's family; now, the idea horrified her.

Jacy entered the glittering room on Leo's arm, and
hesitated slightly at the sight before her. At the end of
the room, on a raised dais, was a typical Greek quartet,
playing ethnic music with great verve. A quick glance
around the rest of the room showed her that every
woman present was dressed to impress. Designer gowns
everywhere.

She breathed deeply. She had been right to splash out
on her Diane Freis, and she gave thanks for the fact that
in her job she'd become adept at mixing with the super-
wealthy—for quite a few of her cases had been the theft
or loss of jewellery collections insured by Mutual, and
in one or two instances the owners themselves had been
responsible.

A waiter appeared in front of them, and spoke to Leo.
Tilting her head a notch, Jacy walked confidently at
Leo's side, smiling politely as he addressed a variety of
friends with a Greek greeting, while the waiter preceded
them to a table for eight at the far side of the room.

'Leo, so glad you could make it.' A short, heavy-set
man arose from his seat at the table that was already
occupied by five other people—three women and two
more men. 'And who is your charming companion?' The
small dark man turned sparkling black eyes towards Jacy.

Leo, with a brilliant smile, urged her forward. 'My
Uncle Nick, and this is Jacy, a very special friend of
mine.'

She held out her hand and it was engulfed in a broad
fist. The next few moments were taken up in a flurry of
introductions. She accepted a seat next to Nick, with
Leo at her other side. She quickly logged in her mind
the various names. Apparently the pretty dark girl opposite was Nina, Nick's daughter, whose birthday it was.
Beside her was a handsome young man, her fiancé,

whose name Jacy missed. Then Nick's wife, Anna, a
rather heavy lady. But it was the last couple that was the
real shock to Jacy: Leo's father and mother. His father
was a carbon copy of his uncle Nick—short and dark,
with a keen intelligence in his black eyes. But Mrs
Kozakis was a tall, angular woman, impeccably gowned
in black with a fantastic diamond necklace around her
throat that must have cost a fortune. One look at the
older woman's face and it was obvious whom Leo
favoured. The features that were ruggedly attractive on
a man somehow made the woman austere and vaguely
forbidding in appearance.

'All right, Jacy?' Leo's breath feathered against her
ear as he bent his dark head towards her. 'Don't be in-
timidated, they won't eat you.'

'I'm not,' she snapped back.

'Drink your wine and watch your temper,' he
prompted, his hard thigh pressing against hers under the
table as if in warning.

The contact was like an electric shock down the length
of her leg; she could feel the colour rising in her face as
she swiftly moved her leg, at the same time lifting the
crystal glass in front of her and taking a long swallow
of the wine. Luckily, no one seemed to notice her mo-
mentary distress—except Leo. With a sardonic glance at
her flushed face he murmured so that only she could
hear, 'Don't overdo the shy act, Jacy; we both know
what we want.'

She almost choked on the wine, and then had to grit
her teeth to prevent herself swearing at the conceited
swine. By the time she had regained control of her
temper, the conversation was flowing around her in
quick-fire Greek.

The meal that followed was typical Greek fare, and
to Jacy's surprise she actually enjoyed it. As course followed course and the wine flowed freely she found herself

quite readily accepted by Leo's family. In fact, if she hadn't known what an immoral animal Leo was she could quite easily have been fooled into believing that he genuinely cared for her.

Replacing her wine glass on the table, having drained it, she frowned slightly. It might be a happy family party but she must never forget she wasn't part of it. Leo had asked her out for a *good time*, a brief fling while he was in London. He had been bluntly honest about it at Liz's party. Her *own* reason for going out with Leo was no more laudable than his: a bet! And she couldn't help thinking that revenge would be sweet... Engrossed in her thoughts, she was unaware that Leo's father had spoken to her.

'Jacy. I asked if you would care to dance?'

At the sound of her name, she lifted her head and with an apologetic smile she answered the older man. 'Yes, please.'

'Tell me, Jacy,' Leo's father asked quietly as he propelled her in a perfect turn to an old fashioned waltz, 'how long have you known my son?'

'Years,' she replied lightly.

'Ah, that would explain why he brought you here tonight. Obviously you are different—a lady friend of long-standing, no?'

Jacy was beginning to feel uncomfortable under the direct gaze of the older man. 'Sort of,' she responded non-committally.

'Do you intend to marry my son?'

The directness of the question staggered her. Her golden eyes widened in shocked surprise, and then twinkled with a touch of humour. 'Good God, no,' she laughed. 'Whatever gave you that idea?'

'We will see,' he replied enigmatically, and as the music ended led her back to the table.

'What has my father been saying to you?' Leo demanded as soon as she sat down. 'You were laughing.'

But before she could reply to his question a laughing Nick was grabbing his arm and something was said in a flurry of Greek. As Jacy looked on in surprise Leo and his father, Uncle Nick and the good looking young man all shed their jackets and ties and, in a group, walked on to the dance-floor.

The next ten minutes were a revelation to Jacy. The band started playing a slow Greek tune. The four men, arms linked at shoulder height, began moving with slow deliberation to the firm beat of the music. Jacy's eyes were drawn to Leo and she couldn't look away.

His brown eyes flashed wickedly and a broad grin curved his handsome face. His chest heaved, the muscles rippling beneath the fine silk of his shirt as the music gradually speeded up. The rest of the party began to clap in time to the music, all eyes fixed on the four men, dancing in a wild, weaving snake across the smooth floor in perfect time to the music.

Jacy couldn't contain a gasp of pure feminine appreciation at the picture the men presented. It should have been effeminate, but the opposite was true. Her golden eyes traced down the length of Leo; his dark trousers were snug on his suggestively swaying hips, the muscles of his thighs bulging beneath the soft fabric. She could feel the heat rise in her face and her eyes were glued to the stunning masculine vibrancy of Leo's tall form. A hot flush of feminine arousal flashed through her body, and she gasped as a plate flew through the air to break at his feet.

He was laughing out loud while never missing a step of the now frenzied pace of the music. Plates were thrown from all sides at the energetic dancers, smashing into smithereens on the hard floor.

Jacy swallowed hard; there was something so primitive, so basically pagan but undeniably sexual about the dance. She sighed, a long, low expulsion of air as the music finally stopped. She hadn't even been aware that she'd been holding her breath. Leo strode towards her, the sweat glistening on his brow, his short dark hair curling damply on his forehead. Rivulets of perspiration ran down his strong throat to mingle in the matt of black hair on his chest. In the exertion of the dance his shirt had come unbuttoned almost to his waist.

The crowd were shouting what she supposed were congratulations in Greek, but her eyes never left the approaching man. She was transported back in time to Corfu and her fisherman lover. Leo looked years younger and just as she remembered him from the first time they'd met.

His glittering, triumphant gaze caught and held hers, and with a panther-like speed he was at her side. His dark head swooped down and, with one hand at the back of her head, he kissed her firmly on her softly parted lips. For a second she made no demur, lost in a sensual haze of years ago. But suddenly the noise around her, and the sound of Leo's name being shouted, made her stiffen in instant rejection. It was too late, though, as Leo, chucking her under the chin with one finger, said, 'Nice, but I need privacy for what I have in mind. Shall we go?'

Blushing furiously, her lips still tingling from his openly possessive kiss, she glanced wildly around the room. Leo's family—aunts, uncles, cousins, the whole lot—seemed to be grinning at her. Leo urged her to her feet and before she knew it they had said their goodbyes and were walking out into the night air. She took a few deep breaths as they waited for the valet to bring the car. She was much too susceptible to Leo's powerful masculinity, and the clasp of his hand around her wrist was checking her pulse-rate, she was sure. She glanced sideways and caught the look of glittering anticipation in his eyes, and her heart shuddered.

In the car, she rested her cheek against the cold glass of the side-window. She didn't understand herself at all. For years she'd been all but immune to members of the opposite sex. She had dated, true, but she had always been in control. Tonight, in a few short minutes, watching Leo dance had aroused all her latent sensual emotions with a ferocity that had left her shocked and trembling.

'To a night club?' Leo asked shortly. 'Or home?'

'Home, please,' Jacy replied as the powerful car sped quickly through the darkened streets. She was tired, emotionally distraught, though she hated to admit as much. Leo was having just as powerful an effect on her senses tonight as he'd had years ago, and she would have to be the biggest idiot alive to think for even one second that she could possibly get the better of such a man. Did she even want to? she asked herself wryly. And the answer was no. Whatever had been between them in the past was long since dead. There was certainly no future for them. Leo wanted a roll in the hay, to put it crudely— and she should have had more sense than to encourage him. The problem was, her body had a completely different idea; she seemed to be plunging like a heat-seeking missile to its target—and the target was Leo.

'Overall I think it was a very good evening.' His deep voice broke into her troubled thoughts. 'My family liked you, and you appeared to get along with them very well.'

Jacy swung around in her seat to look at him, and in that instant she recognised her surroundings. The car had stopped at her own front door. 'You're lucky. You have a lovely family,' she said huskily, and, finding the passenger door-handle, she opened it and stepped out, then started walking towards her front door.

Leo appeared at her side just as she was fitting the key into the lock.

'Such haste; I'm flattered.' Taking the key from her shaking fingers, he opened the door.

'Thank you for a lovely evening, and goodnight,' she shot hurriedly, and made to dash into the house.

'Not so fast, Jacy.' His hand caught her elbow, and before she could protest they were both in the hall and Leo was closing the door behind them. 'Dancing is hot work; I'm looking forward to our chilled champagne,' he drawled silkily, urging her forward.

She stood still, and he paused to look down at her, his height dark and intimidating in the dimly lit hall. 'I would rather you left; I'm very tired.'

'In a few minutes. You wouldn't deprive a thirsty man of refreshment, would you?' he enquired mockingly.

She gave him a grudging, 'OK,' and preceded him through the living room to the kitchen. The light of challenge in his dark eyes was enough to warn her that the simplest course of action was to give him the drink and then get rid of him. That way he would have no excuse to return for his damned champagne! she thought, finally practising some caution. She reached for the handle of the refrigerator, and was stopped by a large, tanned hand catching hers.

'Go and sit down, Jacy. I'll bring it through.'

'You don't know where the glasses are kept,' she argued, reluctant to have him take charge.

'I'll find them. Do as you're told,' he commanded, lifting his other hand to the nape of her neck and urging her around.

Meekly she walked back into the living-room and sat down on the sofa, rubbing the back of her neck with her hand. She was tired, she told herself, and the tension down her spine had absolutely nothing to do with the lingering effect of Leo's touch...

She watched him warily as, within seconds, he appeared with two glasses in one hand and the champagne bottle in the other. With a minimum of fuss the glasses were placed on the low table in front of her, and the champagne expertly opened with a satisfying pop and then poured into the waiting glasses.

'You should have been a waiter,' Jacy remarked as she took the glass Leo offered her, while carefully avoiding touching his fingers.

His dark gaze flashed from her face to her hand and back to her face, as good as telling her that he had noticed her not so subtle avoidance of his touch; but he said nothing. Instead he smiled broadly, picked up his own brimming glass, and sat down beside her.

'I was a waiter for quite some time, and a very good one.'

'A waiter? I don't believe you!' she exclaimed.

'It's perfectly true,' he confirmed, and, casually leaning back, stretching his long legs out in front of him, he raised his glass to his mouth and drank the sparkling wine.

She watched the muscles in his throat move beneath the bronzed skin as he swallowed, and had to swallow herself. He was a dangerously attractive man, and he was much too close for comfort. Hastily Jacy drained her own glass as Leo continued conversationally, 'My father is a firm believer in starting at the bottom and working one's way up. When I was young, our business was not so diversified as it is now. We owned a few hotels and a shipping line. So as a boy of fifteen I was put to work in one of our hotels—then every summer after that until I was twenty-one and had finished university.

'That accounts for your expertise with the bottle,' Jacy said, for the moment forgetting her dislike of the man. Fascinated by this insight into his youth, she unconsciously began to relax in his presence.

'Yes, but I was not always so efficient. I can remember one summer, my first time serving in the dining-room, and I asked a lady if she wanted more hollandaise sauce. The lady was wearing a very low-cut summer dress, and I was momentarily distracted and inadvertently poured the sauce down her shoulder.'

'Oh, no,' Jacy chuckled.

Leo flashed her a quick grin. 'It wasn't funny, I can tell you. It turned out that the scrap of a dress had a designer label, and my father made me pay for it. I worked the whole of the summer for that damn dress.'

Jacy burst out laughing. 'I wish I could have seen you,' she declared, all her antagonism vanishing under the warm smile in Leo's dark eyes.

'I was a skinny teenager, you wouldn't have liked me. But the episode did teach me a valuable lesson.'

'What was that?' she asked, still smiling.

Leaning forward, Leo placed his glass on the table and slid his arm around her shoulders. His dark eyes held hers, his gleaming with devilment. 'I never ogled the female guests ever again. But, I have to say, if ever a garment was made for ogling it's a bustier. I am having the greatest difficulty keeping my eyes off it, and no luck at all with my hand.' As he spoke his free hand lifted, his long fingers tracing along the soft swell of her breast above the beaded cups of her bustier.

Jacy, from being relaxed, was instantly tense. The touch of his fingers on her soft flesh was like a ribbon of fire and she jerked upright, instantly on the defensive; pushing his marauding hand away, she jumped to her feet. 'Obviously you never learned the lesson well enough,' she said drily. 'And I think it's time you left.'

'But we haven't finished the bottle.' His dark eyes gleamed wickedly up at her as he lounged back against the soft cushions of the sofa. 'I can remember the last

time we shared a bottle of champagne, and we finished
it off with you curled on my lap.'

'Did we? I don't remember.' She *did* remember, all
too well, and she also remembered how that night had
ended with Leo storming out. This time it was her turn
to call a halt. 'You're driving, you can't have any more.'

'Come and sit down and share the champagne. If I'm
over the limit for driving I'm sure that, as a gracious
hostess, you will give me a bed for the night.'

'No way,' she shot back, hovering over him, willing
him to get up and go. The thought of Leo anywhere near
her bedroom was enough to send warning signals to every
nerve in her body.

'Frightened, Jacy?' Reaching up, he grabbed her wrist
and with one swift tug she found herself back on the
sofa, and curved into Leo's side.

'Let go...'

'Don't worry, Jacy. I don't go in for rape: subtle persuasion is more my style.'

'And you're always successful, if the Press is to be
believed,' she flung back tautly, and saw his eyes narrow
fractionally in a brief flash of anger.

'I was with you!' he shot back mockingly, and, cap-
turing her chin in one of his hands, he turned her face
towards his. For a long moment his intent gaze lingered
over her beautiful features.

Jacy stiffened with tension and, paradoxically, something more—a heady anticipation of the kiss she was
sure was to follow. But she was wrong.

Leo, holding her eyes with his, declared arrogantly,
'And I will be again, and we both know it.' One long
finger mockingly tapped her full lips as he added, 'But
I'm not so crass that I can't appreciate a little conversation over a fine bottle of champagne first... To old
friends, together...' He raised his glass and drank. 'Join
me, hmm?'

It was the *together* that bothered her. With his muscular thigh pressed against hers and the warmth of his hand cupping her chin, it was oh, so easy to forget how he had hurt her and to relax into his masculine warmth. But his conceited conviction that she would fall into his arms like a ripe plum stiffened her resolve to teach him a lesson. 'I seem to remember your saying the other night that you had a month in town and fancied a good time.' She drawled the last two words deliberately. 'Old friends we are not . . . Or is this another ploy in your subtle persuasion technique?'

'What do you think?' he asked sardonically, his hand falling from her face. He reached out and picked up the wine bottle, and topped up both their glasses. 'And while you're considering, how about a different toast?' Offering her a glass, he raised his own. 'To old lovers and new friends,' he drawled mockingly.

'*Possible* friends,' she amended lightly, and sipped the wine.

'Possibly a friend, but certainly a lover . . . Yes, I'll drink to that.' Leo drained his glass and replaced it on the table, and, turning sideways on the sofa, his fingers brushed hers as he took the empty glass from her hand and put it down with the other.

Fury or fervour flooded her face at the picture his words evoked. She closed her eyes briefly, fighting for control of her wayward emotions. She wanted to slap his mocking features and yet he only had to touch her to set every cell in her body alight.

'Blushing, Jacy? You're an odd girl—beautiful, intelligent, and yet at times tonight, and now this minute, you look like the shy young teenager I once knew.' His brown eyes smouldered with a deepening gleam as they held hers captive. 'Odd, I know. You are an intrepid investigator for your firm and have travelled world-wide

for them. India, wasn't it, last month? And you un-
covered some chemical-factory arson?'

Jacy's eyes widened in amazement. 'How did you
know that?' she blurted unthinkingly.

'I had you investigated. A man in my position can't
be too careful,' he said with dry cynicism. 'You may not
have followed your father into journalism, but you have
obviously inherited his investigative instincts. One would
hope with more honesty...'

She was on her feet in a flash, fury winning. 'How
dare you have me investigated? Of all the bloody nerve!
Do you do that with all your dates? My God, it must
be an expensive exercise.' She couldn't believe the audacity of the man, or his snide remark about her father.

'Calm down, Jacy.' Rising to his feet, he grasped her
upper arm. 'It was nothing personal.'

'Nothing personal?' she parrotted. 'Delving into my
private life!'

A cynical grin spread over his handsome face. 'Actually, I didn't have much luck there. You appear to be
very discreet with your lovers—a good thing. But I am
curious as to how a young woman can afford a house
to herself in central London. You must have had some
wealthy bed-fellows.'

'Get out, just get out,' she cried, her temper ex-
ploding. He still thought of her as little better than a
whore and yet he was quite happy to make love to her
as a brief diversion while he was in London. If she had
needed further proof of what an immoral swine he was,
he had just supplied it. She swung her free arm up to
swipe his grinning face, but he caught her wrist in mid-
air, his long fingers digging into her flesh.

'Such passion should be reserved for the bedroom,
Jacy.' And he actually had the gall to laugh. 'Come on...
You're a woman of the world, and we both know the

score. I don't mind a little feminine reluctance for modesty's sake, but violence——' his grip relaxed slightly on her arm '—isn't my scene, so quit pretending. And don't worry, sweetheart, you won't find me ungenerous...'

His black head descended while she was speechless with rage at his assumption and conceit. But it didn't stop her heart-beat accelerating until it shot out of control as his mouth took hers in a deep, hard kiss. She closed her eyes helplessly, and subtly the kiss changed as he felt her surrender to a long and languorous seduction of her senses, filling her with a warmth that made her mind spin. She only regained her senses as he drew back, and she felt herself swept off her feet.

'Put me down.' She began to struggle so he complied, dropping her on to the sofa and following her down. She lay winded for a second—and Leo wasn't even breathing heavily, she noted bitterly. But then he was a superbly fit male, it was evident in every move he made. He sat on the edge of the sofa, one arm along the back and the other placed firmly on her breast-bone, pinning her down.

'I find your behaviour intriguing,' he pondered, and the very softness of his tone sounded like a threat to Jacy's overstretched nerves. His dark head bent lower and the musky male scent of him teased her nostrils as his mouth covered hers yet again. She was helpless to resist the potent intimacy of his kiss, and slowly all the anger drained out of her, to be replaced with a burning frustration. She wanted to reach up to him, stroke the close-cropped hair, bury her head in the warmth of his neck. But with a terrific effort of will she kept her hands at her sides, her fingers curling into fists.

He raised his head, his brown eyes speculative on her flushed face and desire-hazed eyes. 'I could make love to you now; I could have you begging in minutes.' He traced the soft curve of her breast and watched her tremble helplessly. 'But tell me, I'm curious. Why did you accept my invitation? I made it obvious I wanted you. We are two consenting adults, and yet you're trying your utmost to pretend indifference...' He glanced at her clenched fists. 'Why?' he demanded hardly.

She made no response. She couldn't, she was fighting to control the heavy thumping of her heart.

'It's been apparent all evening that you can barely hide your resentment,' he tagged on musingly.

She lowered her lashes over her golden eyes to mask her expression from the far too astute Leo. Fool, she thought hollowly. Revenge was a stupid idea, and she was far too aware of the man for her little plot ever to have worked. Forcing herself to think sensibly for the first time in half an hour, she hit on the solution for her erratic behaviour and a way to get rid of Leo all in one go. Raising her eyes, she looked up into his dark, knowledgeable face.

'I'm sorry, Leo. I should have cancelled our date.' She hesitated. 'A touch of PMT the past couple of days, and now...' She let her voice trail off...

'You poor darling, you should have told me.' And she was instantly enfolded in his strong arms, her head pressed against his broad chest in a comforting hug. Then he eased her back on the soft cushions, and his brown eyes gleamed down on her small face.

She had to suppress the hysterical laughter that bubbled in her throat at the look of tenderness tinged with pure masculine relief in his expression. 'Stay where you are and I'll make you a hot drink... Then I'll call a cab. All right?'

She smiled her thanks. His easy acceptance of her excuse was comical. But so like Leo—his ego couldn't stand the thought of any woman refusing him; it was much simpler for him to accept that it was the wrong time of the month for her. God, but the man's ego was monumental, Jacy thought wryly, sinking gratefully into the sofa. It might even be interesting to see how he would avoid making a date with her for the next week. He was a man of carnal appetites, and as she was out of commission he would have to find his relief somewhere else . . .

CHAPTER FIVE

BUT her supposition was wrong. Ten days later Jacy stood before the mirror in the bathroom of Leo's opulent London apartment in Eton Square, and surveyed her reflection. Tonight she had opted for the casual look— a plaid skirt in autumn shades, topped with a tangerine silk shirt. It should have clashed with her hair, which was brushed loose around her shoulders in soft curls, but somehow it worked. Huge eyes, wide and luminous, reflective, stared back at her and she barely recognised herself. She had excused herself to go to the bathroom in a last-ditch attempt to regain control of the fluttering nervous anticipation that was tying her stomach in knots, and it was all Leo's fault. At this very minute he was sprawled on the sofa in the lounge, waiting for her to join him, having just dismissed for the night the couple who'd served the intimate dinner they had shared. For the life of her she couldn't understand how she had got herself in this position with a man she had despised for the past ten years.

She reviewed the past week in her mind and to her surprise she was forced to admit that Leo Kozakis had been the most attentive and charming companion. On the Sunday after the party at the Ritz, he had called around to collect his car, and insisted on Jacy joining him for lunch. Monday evening he had escorted her to the latest musical in the West End; Wednesday it was the opening of a new art gallery—one that Leo had an interest in, she had discovered on talking to the young man whose paintings were on exhibition in the place.

Saturday night it had been an intimate dinner at the re-
nowned celebrity restaurant, the San Lorenzo in
Knightsbridge.

A worried frown marred her smooth brow. It was
Sunday evening and he'd suggested a relaxed, lazy night
at his apartment. The trouble was, she thought uncom-
fortably, although Leo had behaved impeccably, her own
behaviour she had difficulty coming to terms with. She
kept telling herself that it was the bet, and a desire for
revenge, that had made her accept his invitations; but
her own innate honesty forced her to admit that neither
reason was the total truth. The bottom line was—she
enjoyed Leo's company. At eighteen she hadn't really
known the man on an intellectual level, but this past
week she had delighted in his conversation, his sharp
intellect, and surprisingly she'd discovered that they had
a lot of common interests, from painting to music and
a love of 'whodunnit' books...

She tried reminding herself that he was a womaniser,
but it didn't stop her heart beating faster when she met
him, or defuse the sexual tension that constantly sim-
mered just beneath the surface when they were together.
His dark eyes lingered on her shapely body, the brief
kisses they shared on parting, were subtle reminders to
Jacy that Leo was a virile, intensely physical male—and
that he wanted her. The lie she had told over a week ago
had protected her so far, but she had an uneasy feeling
tonight that Leo intended a lot more than a goodnight
kiss.

Straightening her shoulders, she took a deep breath
and exhaled slowly, and, fixing a polite smile on her face,
she opened the door of the luxurious bathroom and
walked straight into the hard wall of a very masculine
chest. A pair of strong arms wrapped around her, holding
her steady.

'I was beginning to think you'd got lost.' Leo murmured the words against the top of her head.

Jacy eased back. He was dressed casually in comfortable hip-hugging designer jeans and a soft, baggy blue chambray shirt, open at the neck to reveal an enticing glimpse of crisp, curling body hair. She swallowed hard and, tilting her head, looked up into his ruggedly attractive face.

'Are you all right now?' he demanded huskily, not trying to hide the avid hunger in his gaze. His brown eyes, dilated to almost black, captured hers and she had the sinking feeling that he was not asking her solely about the shock of bumping into him.

Jacy could feel the heavy beat of his heart beneath the small hand she had defensively splayed across his chest. She felt the heat building in her lower stomach, the warmth of his muscular thighs hard against the soft wool of her skirt, and she chewed her lip nervously, unable to answer him. The problem was that her own feelings were no longer so clear-cut. Her *head* said she should despise him, but she was beginning to realise that it would be a very simple step to being completely enthralled by him all over again, and the thought terrified her.

'Yes, I'm fine,' she managed to respond in what she hoped was a cool tone, but the huskiness of her voice betrayed her conflicting emotions.

'In that case, my bedroom's next door,' Leo said thickly, his eyes grazing over her upturned face and lower to the enticing cleavage revealed by the V-neck of her silk shirt, then lower still to her narrow waist, the soft feminine curves of her hips, and her flat stomach. His fascinated gaze fed on every inch of her before slowly drifting up to her mouth and finally to her wide, honey-gold eyes.

She swallowed hard. An image of her younger self and Leo, naked limbs entwined, flashed into her mind, and she felt light-headed at the thought of once more experiencing the potent force of Leo's lovemaking. But that way lay madness, she reminded herself, all her defensive instincts coming to the fore. He wanted her, but wanting wasn't enough for the mature Jacy. Or was it, when every nerve-end in her body cried out for fulfilment?

'Still the same egocentric Leo,' she said tightly, trying to defuse the atmosphere of electric tension surrounding them. Pushing against his chest, she made to slip past him.

His expression snapped from hungry need to puzzled bewilderment. 'What are you playing at?' he countered hardly, one hand sliding down from her shoulder to slip loose a button of her shirt, his thumb brushing the swell of her breasts.

She gasped and inhaled sharply at the contact, her hand reaching to cover his. 'Don't!'

'Why not? We have spent the last week together and I've made it perfectly clear that I want you, and you know you want me; the chemistry between us is as powerful as ever.' Deliberately his fingers played with the fastening of her shirt, teasingly brushing her breasts. 'You're no shy young virgin, and I should know,' he drawled mockingly, his glance dipping to where her hand ineffectively rested on his and then back to her face, fully aware of her obvious response to his caress.

Jacy quivered. He was right, damn him! But she had no intention of admitting as much, certainly not after his last crack. 'I don't go in for one-night stands,' she protested, fighting down the incredible urge to lean into his hard, hot body.

'It could never be a one-night stand for us, Jacy,' he declared throatily. And, as if losing all patience, his fingers tightened around hers at her breast and he hauled her against him, trapping their joined hands between them while his other arm encircled her waist, his hand stroking suggestively up her spinal cord. 'We've been lovers before and we will be again. I've tried to be reasonable,' he mouthed against the top of her head. 'How I've stopped myself from touching you these past few days is a miracle of self-control. I'm not trying to rush you, Jacy——' his grip tightened around her slender waist '—but celibacy doesn't suit me.' And with his other hand he raised hers to his shoulder and placed it there before dropping his hand back to the opening of her shirt and burrowing beneath one soft, silk-cupped, lacy-clad breast. 'Or you either, by the look of things.' His dark eyes were fixed on her hardening breast, his voice thick. 'Don't try to deny it. You want me.'

'No,' Jacy murmured, but with little conviction, unable to resist his intimate touch as heat-waves of desire coursed down her spine. He moved his thighs restlessly against her, the hard heat of his masculine arousal pulsing against her abdomen. The fact that she could so easily arouse him fuelled her own growing excitement. Her body, with a will of its own, arched into his, but as his head bent to find her mouth a last thread of self-preservation had her turning away to avoid his kiss. Was she such a fool as to fall again for the same suggestive talk and hard body?

'Don't play games with me, Jacy,' he said thickly, a sharp edge of angry frustration in his voice. 'I'm too old and too experienced for teasing females.'

'I'm not playing games,' she got out shakily.

'No? Then come to bed,' he demanded arrogantly. 'You know you want to.'

It was his supreme arrogance that finally gave her the strength to pull out of his arms and dash into the lounge.

Leo followed, grabbing her wrist before she could reach the entrance-hall and escape.

'What the hell is the matter with you?' he asked furiously. 'Do you make a habit of leading men on? Is that something you've learnt in the past ten years?' His eyes darkened as he looked down at her. 'I'm nobody's fool, and I don't take kindly to frustration...'

'My God, you've some nerve,' Jacy flung back at him, her mature sophistication flying out of the window as her barely controlled emotions were overtaken by a rush of anger. 'You think a few dinners and a show entitle you to a woman's body... well, let me tell you, buster— not *this* woman's. The last ten years have taught me to be a lot more discerning than the young girl you seduced. When and if I have a lover I will want a hell of a lot more than a couple of dates and into bed.'

'My apologies,' Leo said in a menacing voice. 'I forgot for a moment that all women have a price. What's yours—a diamond bracelet? Or perhaps you'd prefer a necklace? No wonder you own a house in London; you've used your body well. But if it's marriage you're holding out for, don't hold your breath.'

He had regained his cool control with an insulting ease that infuriated her and underscored how little he actually thought of her. She swung her arm in a smooth arc, her hand connecting resoundingly with his tanned cheek. 'And to think I thought I'd misjudged you, that perhaps you weren't the lecherous liar I had you pegged for,' she spat disgustedly. 'My father was right about you.' She stopped suddenly, afraid of what she might reveal in her angry panic, and appalled at how quickly the anger had flared between them.

The silence that followed her outburst lengthened until the tension was almost tangible. Jacy raised her eyes to Leo's darkly flushed face, noting the imprint of her hand on his tanned skin, and then her eyes met his and she flinched beneath the indomitable anger in their black depths.

'I won't retaliate in kind, not this time.' He hauled her hard against him, his arm around her waist, and with his other hand forced her chin up so she had to face him. 'Because I think that, at last, we are getting to the truth,' he said softly but with a deadly intent. 'You're a sophisticated lady, a delightful companion, and yet all week I have sensed a certain antagonism just below the surface of your so charming exterior.'

Unfortunately for Jacy, she couldn't stop the guilty colour flooding her face; he was much closer to the truth than he realised. 'I don't know what you mean.' She tried to shrug but his arm tightened around her, his hand at her chin sliding to circle her neck, his thumb resting on the pulse that beat erratically in her throat.

'Oh, I think you do. You're twenty-eight, not eighteen any more.' His smile was chilling. 'There have been other men in your life, other lovers over the years, so why this pretence of outraged virtue? It doesn't become you, Jacy. You might try to fool yourself but you can't fool me. I can recognise a sexually aroused woman and I know you're burning with the same sexual frustration I feel.'

If only he knew, she thought helplessly, frightened of the way her body reacted to him. Her knees felt weak and her heart thudded. She lowered her lashes to block out the intense speculation in his dark gaze. He had spoiled her for any other man. Only Leo brought forth this aching response in her traitorous body.

'You mentioned your father,' he said so slowly that she could almost hear the cogs in his brilliant mind ticking over. 'And my womanising ways.'

Jacy flicked a glance up at him and was suddenly wary of the speculative gleam in his eyes.

He laughed softly, his fingers relaxing on her throat and stroking gently. 'Now I get it,' he drawled huskily,

obviously having reached a satisfactory assessment of
the situation in his own mind. 'You think I'm still carrying a grudge against your father. Is that it, sweetheart?'
he asked encouragingly, his eyes defying her to look away
from him. 'Well, forget it—I don't give a damn about
the past and, anyway, the man is dead.' He bent his head
and pressed his lips to the pulse beating madly at the
base of her throat. 'Come on, Jacy, you know you want
to. Take a gamble on me and I'll bet you will enjoy it.'
His teeth bit lightly, teasingly on her neck. 'I won't hurt
you. At least, not intentionally,' he added, his voice rich
with sensual meaning.

Jacy was stunned into immobility. That he could come
up with such a suggestion just about took the biscuit,
and his mention of gambling rang oddly sinister in her
ears. Leo couldn't possibly know about her bet, could
he? She flushed furiously and jerked her head back,
fighting down the fierce tide of pleasure that surged
through her veins at his caress.

'*You* carrying a grudge against *me*?' she said
scathingly. 'You've got to be joking. Shouldn't that be
the other way around?' She was positively sizzling with
anger and resentment. 'As I recall, you walked out on
me after feeding me a pack of lies about being a poor
fisherman. You—the high and mighty Kozakis—filling
in a few weeks with a naïve teenager while your lawyers
were blackening some poor innocent ex-girlfriend's name
back in America.'

It would have been funny if it weren't so tragic, Jacy
thought as Leo stepped back, his arms falling by his sides
and an expression of shocked amazement on his face.
It had obviously never occurred to him that she might
consider he was at fault. She was free, but she was also
furious.

'Really, Leo, you have a hell of a selective memory.
You called me worse than a whore, and you actually

expect me to forgive and forget——' flinging out her arm, she snapped her fingers in his face '—just like that?'

Leo swung on his heel and crossed the room to stand in front of the elegant Georgian window, his back to Jacy. He savagely pulled a cord and the heavy cream velvet drapes slid back to reveal the flickering glow of the street lights of London.

Jacy saw his dark head shake slightly. His broad shoulders looked oddly taut. She knew that now was her chance to leave, walk out and never see Leo again; but for some reason her feet were reluctant to move. Her gaze wandered around the room, lingering on the huge, over-stuffed, soft cream hide sofa and its smaller matching counterpart, then moved on to the ornate marble fireplace, the functional antique walnut desk and occasional table, where coffee-cups and the glasses and bottle of wine that they'd shared half an hour earlier still stood, looking somehow intimate.

A crack jerked her attention back to the man who stood by the window. Leo, one hand balled into a fist, slapped the palm of his other hand. 'My God, I never realised...' He stopped, but Jacy knew that he hadn't been speaking to her. Suddenly he swung back around, his dark eyes clashing with hers.

For a second Jacy could have sworn she saw pain etched into his handsome features, but it vanished as his dark brows drew together in an angry scowl as he searched her pale face with unwavering scrutiny. Nervously she ran her damp palms down over her slender hips and, unable to hold his gaze, dropped her eyes to stare at the floor.

'Now I understand, Jacy. This past week has been your way of seeking revenge for what you obviously saw as my scornful treatment of you in the past,' he said icily.

'No, of course not,' she denied, but her denial didn't carry much conviction.

'How long did you think you could string me along with the promise of your body?' he asked silkily. 'A month?'

Her head shot up; why had he picked a month? 'No, I never thought...I...' She stopped, eyeing him warily as he walked towards her.

He placed his large hands on her shoulders. 'You never thought... Yes, I can believe that. In my experience, women rarely do.' She almost sighed with relief, but then was stunned as he continued, 'I never realised until tonight how I might have hurt you by my furious outburst years ago.' Like a sheep she allowed him to lead her to the sofa and pull her down beside him. One strong arm rested on her slender shoulders. She stiffened at the enforced intimacy, then relaxed as he said, 'We need to talk... You were very young, and perhaps I *was* a little hard on you. Maybe I treated you shabbily. But it was a difficult time for me.'

Maybe! There was no maybe about it... And *he* had been having a difficult time? What about her? Jacy wanted to ask. She couldn't see Leo ever finding life difficult: he strode through it with money and power and a blatant masculine chauvinism that prevented anything or anyone ever hurting him... She glanced sideways at him. '*You*, in difficulties—I don't believe it's possible,' she said drily.

'I know. I didn't think it was possible either, but I can assure you it did happen.'

Her lips quirked in a grin at the arrogance of his statement. She might have guessed that Leo wasn't the sort to admit to a weakness like lesser mortals. At least not for long.

'I never explain my actions to anyone, but in your case I am willing to make an exception, and then hopefully we can get back to what we really want—each other.'

'Big of you,' she snorted inelegantly.

'Yes, it is rather,' Leo drawled mockingly, and Jacy felt like hitting him. But, guessing her intention, he settled his arm firmly around her shoulder while his free hand caught her hand in his. 'Listen . . .' he said, and she did.

'I don't know how much you know about the trial I was involved in. But, for a start, the lady concerned was no innocent young girl.' His mouth twisted with cynical humour. 'I, on the other hand, was twenty-four, and in America for the first time—sent by my father to head up our business interests there. I met Lily in a nightclub; she was a singer and a good ten years older than me. We were lovers. But I only saw her on my infrequent trips to California, a month or two at most in any one year. Anyway, I had known her for almost two years when she told me she had been thrown out of her apartment, the building having been taken over by a development company, and I, feeling sorry for her, told her that she could stay in the Kozakis company apartment until she found something that suited her. My one mistake.' He shrugged his shoulders. 'I thought it would cost me nothing; in fact, it was a hell of a lot less expensive than the jewellery I used to give her. I wasn't quite as wealthy then. My father was still in charge,' he said with blunt practicality.

Jacy, watching his face, was struck by the hard cynicism in his dark eyes. But she couldn't deny the ring of truth to his words.

'Barely a year later I found out from the security guard at the apartment block, on one of my very rare visits, that not only was Lily entertaining a variety of men, she had also been caught with drugs in her possession. The papers were right, I did throw her out—but I also gave her enough money to lease another apartment. Lily, however, was a greedy lady, and with the compliance of a less than honest lawyer thought she would try to hit me for more money. Hence the palimony case. The one time I acted the gentleman and it cost me dearly—not in money, that didn't matter, but in aggravation. Your father's paper ran the story, and for a few months my life was disrupted...'

Disrupted. Jacy couldn't help smiling. Anyone else would have been traumatised, but not Leo...

'But happily the Court found in my favour and awarded the lady one dollar...'

'One dollar!' Jacy exclaimed. She had never read the newspaper reports; in fact, except for that one night in Corfu, she and her father had never mentioned the subject again: it had been too painful for the younger Jacy to even contemplate. But now she instinctively believed Leo.

'Yes. But the damage to me was much greater. My reputation was worse than mud, and it hurt my family. I don't allow *anyone* to harm my family.' His mouth tightened into a hard line, and he looked somewhere over her head, a remote expression in his dark eyes. Jacy shivered. No one would ever cross this man and live to tell the tale, she knew, and she had been a fool to try...

Leo dropped his gaze to Jacy and regarded her silently for several seconds, then his lips twisted into the beginnings of a smile. 'Then one summer day in Corfu I met you on the beach. A lovely innocent young girl. I didn't lie to you, Jacy. I never actually said I was a fisherman, but it was so refreshing to meet a girl who didn't know who I was or the sordid details of my immediate past. You were a welcome balm to my dented ego.'

Jacy's heart sank. So *that* was what she had meant to him. A young girl to ease his battered ego, nothing more. While she had imagined they were in love...

'The night your father arrived I saw red. He was the editor of the paper that had first run the story, and you were his daughter and a budding reporter. I was so furious, I stormed off.'

'I remember,' she murmured, a lingering sadness tingeing her tone. 'I never had any firm intention of being a reporter, and after your denouncement of the whole breed ... well ...'

'Jacy, I couldn't care less about your work. When I met you again at Liz's party, I saw a beautiful woman and asked you out simply because I want you. It was only tonight when you lashed out at me that I realised how it was possible I might inadvertently have hurt you in the past. So, now that I have put the past in perspective, can we finally get on with the present—and hopefully to bed?'

Leo had been brutally honest with her, and she could understand why he'd behaved the way he had. It must have been very difficult for a man with Leo's supreme confidence to accept the fact that he'd been made a fool of. She could even understand why he'd lashed out at her all those years ago. But what she found harder to accept was his casual assumption that, having explained himself, probably as near an apology as Leo was capable of making, they could swan off to bed!

She pulled herself upright and, perched on the edge of the sofa, she turned her body slightly to look at him. He was lounging back against the sofa, his long legs stretched out in front of him in negligent ease, his hands resting lightly on his thighs, his dark face expressionless. Only a nerve beating beneath the bronzed skin of his cheek told her that he wasn't as relaxed as he was trying to appear.

'So, what's it to be, Jacy? It's up to you,' he prompted tautly.

Her golden eyes searched his dark features. He was a proud man and he had made a great concession in even explaining about his past. He wanted her, and in all honesty Jacy knew she ached for him. But could she be as mature as Leo and forget all her old resentment and bitterness? Take what was on offer—a few weeks of sexual satisfaction—and play the game by his rules? She looked into his eyes and was fascinated by the tinge of uncertainty that even the masculine need blazing fiercely in their depths could not quite disguise.

She could say no! She knew that Leo would accept it—he'd told her last week that violence wasn't his style, but subtle persuasion...

She should say no! Then his thumb traced the vein in her wrist. She saw the black flare of passion in his eyes, and she knew the same emotion was reflected in hers. The decision was made for her; the trembling inside her gave her the answer.

'I believe you're not quite the rat I thought you were,' she murmured teasingly, holding out her other hand, her body swaying towards him as she added, 'And who am I kidding? I'd rather have a tycoon than a fisherman any day.' She knew that it probably only confirmed his less than flattering view of her, but it was better than admitting that she'd loved him years ago, and could quite easily again. He was offering nothing but a brief affair; at the very most she might possibly win her bet, she thought with bitter irony.

Leo caught both her hands and cradled them in his own. Then, in a potently erotic gesture, he kissed the centre of each palm. 'I knew you were a sensible female.' His dark voice was a whisper of rough velvet against her skin as his mouth trailed kisses over her wrist while he gently urged her towards him. 'You won't regret it.'

Sensible was the last thing she was, Jacy admitted, but she could deny the urging of her body no longer. Her gaze fastened on his sensuous mouth and her tongue flicked out unconsciously over her suddenly dry lips.

Dropping her hands, Leo grasped a handful of her hair, his long fingers tangling in the silken gold locks. He urged her face to his. 'Jacy, what are you doing to me?' he groaned, before covering her mouth with his own.

She made a tiny moue of protest before sweetly opening her lips. Leo was inside at once, his tongue tasting, searching, provoking, until she was responding with the intense excitement only Leo could arouse. Jacy raised her arms, her hands sinking into the gleaming thickness of his hair, trailing to curve the nape of his strong neck as the kiss went on and on. She felt the sofa at her back and the pressure of Leo's hard body forcing her down, but she didn't care.

Then Leo raised his head and his dark eyes blazed with masculine triumph as he demanded, 'No turning back this time, Jacy.'

With a soft, throaty groan she linked her hands around his neck and pulled his head back down to hers, her lips giving him the answer he wanted.

The soft silk of her shirt was pushed aside, her front-fastening bra quickly unclasped and her firm, full breasts were freed to his searching hands. When his palm grazed lightly over one nipple, teasing it into a hard peak, Jacy moaned. Leo swallowed her small sound of passion and slid his hand to the other pouting breast. By the time his subtly teasing fingers were finished, Jacy's breasts were achingly sensitive.

Deftly Leo removed the blouse from her shoulders and swung her long legs from the floor across his lap, his hand lingering on the back of her knee. Slowly he stroked up to her thigh and she gasped as his fingers found the naked flesh where her stockings ended. His fingers closed over the tiny lace strap of her garter-belt, and snapped the elastic.

'A welcome addition since last time,' he drawled, but not quite steadily. Straightening, he quickly divested himself of his shirt. His dark head thrown back, he stared down at her. 'Garter-belts turn me on something wicked.' He smiled wolfishly as he studied her naked thighs; her skirt was rucked up around her hips. 'But everything about you turns me on.' His dark eyes deepened to black as he greedily scanned her naked breasts, the hard tips pleading for his caress.

Jacy was enthralled by the sight of his bare torso, the matt of black hair, the glistening bronzed skin. She reached out for him with impatient hands. Her fingers traced through the hair on his chest, over small, flat male nipples until Leo, with a throaty growl, slipped his hand to her waist and eased down the zip of her skirt, his hand slipping downwards over her stomach.

'Leo.' She said his name softly, breathlessly, then his dark head bent and his mouth closed over the turgid point of her breast, licking and nibbling, his teeth lightly grazing first one and then the other. Her arms went around his broad back, her fingers digging into the hard muscle as his other hand found the edge of her panties, his long fingers sliding inside to stroke her hot moist centre...

Jacy clung tightly to the strong, massive bulk of his shoulders as she felt the delicious tremors flood her body. Dear heaven! How had she done without this man, this feeling, for so long? She turned her head into his shoulder and bit into his sleek satin skin with a cat-like savagery.

Leo trailed kisses from her breast to her throat while with a firm hand he urged her thighs apart. 'You're ready for me, Jacy; hot, wet and wanting.' He growled the words, lifting his darkly flushed face to stare down at her softly parted lips. 'And God knows I've been waiting for you long enough,' he rasped, before once more covering her mouth with his own, his fingers still working their indescribable magic.

Jacy whimpered her need as the tension spiralled in her body. She stroked her small hand down over his chest, wanting to give him the same pleasure, and slid her hand down his taut thigh, tracing his hard manhood through the fabric of his trousers. She heard his muffled groan of pleasure while drowning in the musky masculine smell of him, her slender body vibrating with pleasure.

'Jacy, Jacy...' Leo growled, his hand covering hers at his thigh. Then she felt his hand at the snap of his jeans and tried to help him, her fingers grazing his flat belly.

A string of throaty Greek words encouraged her endeavours, as soft moans and sighs interspersed with the long, drugging kisses that he showered on her swollen mouth. She was lost in the molten passion of his desire; she could hear bells ringing in her head and it seemed as if Leo would steal the very breath from her body.

'No, no, no,' Leo grated, his hard thighs grinding her into the sofa. 'I don't believe it.'

Reluctantly he lifted his dark head and rolled off her, sitting on the side of the sofa. His broad shoulders shook as he took great gulping breaths, and only then did Jacy realise that the ringing wasn't in her head but was in fact the strident bell of a telephone, echoing in the heavy, passion-laden atmosphere. 'Ignore it,' she whispered breathily.

Leo turned to stare down at her, at her golden eyes beckoning him back, and he gave a mighty sigh. His sensual mouth twisted in a wry smile of self-mockery. 'I can't—it's the company apartment so it must be business.' He bent and lightly brushed her lips before striding across the room to pick up the offending instrument.

Jacy watched him, mesmerised. His broad back was all rippling muscle and sinew, and his dark hair was mussed in appealing disarray. He was gorgeous...and hers. She tensed and shivered slightly at her thoughts. No. He was not hers. It was lust, pure and simple...

He slammed the phone down and turned back to her. 'I have to go, Jacy. You'd better dress.'

'Yes,' she quietly agreed.

With a ragged sigh Leo ran a hand through his short hair. 'God! I'm sorry, I think I will very probably die of frustration, but unfortunately that was from the shipping office in Athens. One of our cruise-liners is in trouble in mid-Pacific. I'm flying to America immediately; I've got to find out what has gone wrong. The company jet is standing by at Heathrow.'

'Oh, Leo, I'm sorry,' she murmured. But was she? she wondered, carefully pulling on her clothes and smoothing her skirt back down over her hips. Perhaps she needed more time to accept the kind of adult relationship that Leo was offering, and the telephone call was in a way a reprieve. But the screaming frustration of her body didn't appear to agree with her, she thought wryly.

'Not half as sorry as I am,' Leo declared bluntly and, crossing to where she stood, he lifted her chin with one finger and drawled throatily, 'Promise me we can carry on where we left off when I return.'

'Yes, all right,' she said, kissing him teasingly on the nose. This is the best way, she told herself. Keep it light.

His arms closed tightly around her. 'And a word of warning: I insist on an exclusive relationship with my woman—so no other men.'

'There has never been any other man.' The words popped out unconsciously and she felt the tell-tale colour rising in her cheeks.

Leo arched one dark eyebrow sardonically. 'You don't have to go that far, Jacy; just behave yourself from now on.'

She didn't know whether to be glad or sorry that he hadn't believed her, but she had no opportunity to think about it as Leo called her a taxi and saw her into it, his parting words, 'I'll call you tomorrow night.'

CHAPTER SIX

JACY snuggled down under the rose-covered duvet, determined to put Leo out of her head and sleep. But his cool explanation of their past relationship still lingered in her mind. It shouldn't, but it still hurt to have it confirmed that ten years ago he had never loved her. That was obvious from his revelations tonight. She had been a balm to his bruised ego, and that was all... She sighed, and turned restlessly.

Haughty, handsome Leo... He thought he had some God-given right to ride roughshod over lesser mortals, using them when it suited him and discarding them without a second thought. Unfortunately, knowing the ruthless power of the man didn't stop her whole body flushing with heat as she thought of the liberties she had allowed him earlier that evening. Where had her ice-maiden act gone? No man had got to first-base with her in years, but Leo, in one week, had reduced her to a mindless wanton. If the telephone hadn't rung, they would have been lovers—again...

She lifted a finger to her swollen lips, the memory of his kisses still fresh in her mind... Perhaps the maturity of her working life was finally spilling over into her private life, because she knew that she wanted Leo and she was going to wait for him. And was it so wrong? She was a bit old to be hankering after the hearts and flowers, and wedding-bells. It was time she was more realistic, she told herself, and she crushed the tiny voice of conscience reminding her that she wasn't the kind of girl to settle for anything less. With a bit of luck she might even win the bet! With that thought, she fell into a deep, dreamless sleep.

'You're looking remarkably pleased with yourself this morning, Ms Carter. Can I guess why?' Mike, the office junior, stood in front of her desk, a cheeky grin on his freckled face.

'Thank you, Mike. And what are you after?' Jacy responded, looking up from the pile of papers in front of her with a smile. Mike was a dear but he was also always on the dodge; for him to pass a compliment meant that he was after something.

'Nothing, nothing at all. Only I thought you might like to see my newspaper.'

'That rag.' She knew from experience that young Mike had a great interest in the seedier tabloids, which, considering he was a university graduate and supposed to be training as a financial consultant, seemed somewhat out of character. 'You've got to be joking.'

'Oh, I don't know, there's a good photograph of you in it. You can look real sexy when you let your hair down.' He leered suggestively.

Jacy was out of her chair and reaching over the desk to snatch the paper out of his hand in a flash. 'Me... where?' she exclaimed in horror.

Mike laughed out loud. 'Got you that time. Try page five.'

Rapidly she flicked through the pages, and stopped. With a low groan she collapsed back into her chair and spread the offending page on the desk in front of her. There, in glorious Technicolor, was a picture of herself and Leo leaving the restaurant on Saturday night. But it was the caption that brought the colour to her face. 'Leo Kozakis, once noted for always having a glamorous blonde on his arm, but over the past few years becoming adept at avoiding the Press, has returned to the London

scene in style. Miss Jacy Carter, who shared an intimate
dinner with the fabulously wealthy Greek, is not only
beautiful but—my sources in the City tell me—she is
known as a high-flyer in the prestigious firm, the Mutual
Save and Trust company—a directorship is not out of
the question. Quite a change from Kozakis' usual
bimbos. Well done, Leo!'

Of all the patronising, chauvinistic pigs. Jacy swore
at the author under her breath. 'Thank you, Mike,' she
snapped. Rolling the paper up and throwing it at him,
she added, 'Take your rubbish and go.' She was furious
and long after Mike had left her office, closing the door
quietly behind him, she was still burning with resentment. Congratulating Leo! Because she had brains!
What a nerve!

Work—that was what she needed; and, deliberately
returning her attention to the papers in front of her, she
began to read. It was an interesting case. Over the last
six months, five hair-care clinics dotted around the
country had mysteriously caught fire, all owned by the
same firm. The insurance liability was Mutual's but they
were very reluctant to pay, and Jacy could see why. The
thing smelt to high heaven. Half an hour later she had
cooled down enough to call her secretary on the in-
tercom and ask apologetically, 'If you see Mike, Mary,
tell him I'm sorry for yelling, and if it's not too much
trouble can I have a coffee?'

She had over-reacted about the article, she knew. If
she was going to continue seeing Leo she would have to
get used to this kind of scurrilous Press-reporting; but
she couldn't help thinking it was distasteful. Probably
it had been an unfortunate choice of restaurant on
Saturday. It was noted as a favourite of the Royals—not
that there had been any there on Saturday. No doubt
some member of the paparazzi, bored after a fruitless

vigil outside the restaurant, had snapped Leo and Jacy
as better than nothing...

Jacy looked up as her office door opened and Mary,
her secretary, entered with a coffee-cup in her hand and
a broad grin on her plump, friendly face. 'So, tell all,
do. Is Kozakis as good as they say?'

'Not you too, Mary, please.' Taking the cup, Jacy
swallowed thirstily before replacing it on the saucer and
looking up into the laughing blue eyes of her secretary.
'All right, Mary. For the office grape-vine, and to avoid
any exaggeration, yes, I do know Leo Kozakis. I've
known him since I was a teenager and we're just good
friends. Got that?'

'Yes, ma'am! Whatever you say!' She saluted cheekily
and added, 'By the way, Liz rang and said would you
call her back after one?'

Jacy worked through her lunch-hour, only grabbing
a couple of sandwiches from the staff canteen, and,
having eaten them, she reluctantly called Liz. No doubt
her friend had seen the same paper, and wanted a blow
by blow account. But in that she was wrong.

'Hi! Jacy, listen, I can't stop now, I have to dash—
it's my afternoon helping out at the day-nursery. But
I'm coming up to London on Wednesday. Can we meet
for lunch?'

Jacy happily agreed, and arranged the time and place
then spent the rest of the afternoon studying the case
before her. At four a surprising development had her re-
planning her week. A call from the head-office in
Manchester of the hair-care clinic revealed that on the
Sunday night a bottling-plant they owned had been
burned down.

Drastic action was called for, Jacy decided, and after
meeting with her immediate superior, Mr Brown, it was
agreed that she should travel to the north-west at the
earliest opportunity. As she left the office that night Mr

Brown's instructions echoed in her head. 'And don't come back until you've solved it, Jacy.'

A rueful grimace curved her full lips as she drove home. After consulting her desk diary, she realised that the earliest she could get away was Thursday. And where did that leave her relationship with Leo? He would probably be back in London and she would be stuck up in Manchester.

By eleven o'clock that night, Jacy's cautious optimism of the previous evening—that perhaps this time she could handle an adult relationship with Leo Kozakis—had dwindled to nothing. She had hovered over the telephone all night until finally, at midnight, she'd climbed into her lonely bed, calling herself fifty kinds of fool. She had exposed herself to the gutter Press, risked her business reputation, and almost allowed Leo to make love to her again. And all for nothing. She obviously meant no more to him than any other woman he had dated. His promise to call her was just so much guff.

She burrowed down under the duvet and curled up in a little ball, squeezing her eyes shut against the tears that threatened to fall. She had vowed ten years ago not to shed another tear over Leo, and she had held true to that vow until now. She was damned if she was going to weep over the man again, she told herself, but that didn't stop a single drop of moisture easing between her long lashes. With a hard hand she brushed her cheek. Stupid, stupid, stupid, she castigated herself.

Then the telephone rang. In her haste to answer it, her travelling-clock was knocked off the bedside table, but she barely noticed as breathlessly she said, 'Hello...'

'Jacy. Leo here.' His rich, dark voice echoed down the telephone-wire as clear as if he were in the room with her.

Jacy's heart skipped a beat and then raced like crazy.

'Jacy, are you there?' Leo demanded urgently.

'Do you know what time it is?' she blurted, finally managing to speak. 'Almost one in the morning, and I was in the papers today—you as well.' She was babbling but she could not seem to stop. 'I don't...'

'Jacy, calm down and forget about the papers. It means nothing.' Leo cut in hardly and then, in a much softer tone, apologised. 'I'm sorry—I forgot about the time-zone. It's a lovely sunny afternoon in California.'

'It's a miserable wet night here, and I'm in bed.'

'I hope you're alone, and missing me,' Leo drawled softly.

'I'm certainly alone, and as for missing you...' she almost said yes but substituted '...maybe.'

'I suppose I can be content with alone, and maybe,' he responded roughly, satisfaction evident in his tone. 'But the frustration is killing me after last night and what nearly happened. A few more minutes and you would have been mine again. God! I wish I was there with you now.'

'It would be a tight squeeze,' she teased, thinking— keep it light, sophisticated. 'I'm in bed and it's only a single.'

'Oh, I'm sure if I tucked you underneath me we could manage,' he drawled sexily.

Her stomach clenched with an ache of longing so fierce that she groaned out loud, and Leo recognised the sound.

'Don't *do* that, Jacy. Not when I am half a world away and unable to cover your sensuous mouth with mine and swallow those aroused, erotic little noises you make that turn me inside out.'

'Leo, please.'

'Oh, I *will* please you, and that's a promise,' he vowed throatily, and continued to tell her in graphic detail exactly how...

Her breasts hardened in taut arousal, the duvet suddenly too hot to bear against her aching flesh. She flung the cover back and it was all she could do to say softly, 'I don't think you're allowed to say things like that on the telephone.'

A throaty chuckle greeted her comment. 'Playing Miss Prim, Jacy? And yet in my imagination I have a vivid image of you splayed naked on a bed, your golden hair tumbling down over your superb breasts.'

'Leo, enough.' His name came out as a groan; his words turned her on even when he was thousands of miles away.

Triumphant masculine laughter greeted her comment. 'Perhaps you're right. I'm using a public phone in a restaurant. As it is I will have great difficulty walking out of here for the next half-hour.'

She chuckled. 'Serves you right for talking dirty.'

'Talking is about all we can do for the next few days, and you would not want to deprive a man of a vicarious thrill, would you?' he declared with wry mockery.

Some imp of mischief made her reply in a low throaty drawl, 'I wouldn't like to see you deprived of anything.' She dragged out the last word.

'Oh, Jacy, what are you trying to do to me? Let's get down to business quickly, or I shall have to spend the rest of the day in this place.'

Laughing, Jacy sank back down on to the pillow, holding the telephone to her ear and listening intently as Leo described what had happened.

Apparently the cruise-liner wasn't too badly damaged and was limping towards the nearest port, a small island in the Pacific. Leo still had a few loose ends to attend to, but he hoped to be back by Friday.

'But I have to go to Manchester on Thursday, and I don't know how long for,' she told him regretfully, and briefly outlined the case she was working on.

'Not to worry, we'll work something out and I'll call you Wednesday night,' he promised.

By the time they finally broke the connection, Jacy was floating on cloud nine. But half an hour later, lying restlessly in her bed, she was scolding herself for being such a fool. Leo wanted to bed her, nothing more—and she'd better remember that if she wanted to avoid being hurt. Sex was the name of the game, she told herself; and they didn't come any sexier than Leo...

Jacy was still trying to remind herself to keep her feet on the ground, and that it was an adult affair when she strode into the restaurant in Harrods on Wednesday to meet Liz.

'Should I curtsy—given your celebrity status?' A grinning Liz stood up as Jacy approached the table.

'Fool,' she said with a grin and, pulling out a chair, sat down. Liz looked lovely as usual in a winter wool suit in bright red, reminding Jacy of 'Little Red Riding Hood'.

'As long as you're not being a fool as well,' Liz responded quietly, her blue eyes fixing her with steely intent. 'I know I said you should get a man, but Leo Kozakis! Tom showed me the paper with your picture splashed across the gossip column. I didn't expect you to dive in at the deep end—are you sure you can handle it, Jacy? I know you knew him before, and obviously it didn't work out, so...'

Jacy didn't respond immediately, instead she gave her order to the hovering waitress. A smoked salmon salad. 'Have you ordered, Liz?'

'No. Make mine the same—and don't change the subject.'

Jacy sat back in her chair, resigned to revealing at least some of the truth to her friend. 'OK, I met Leo on holiday in Corfu over ten years ago. We had a holiday romance, nothing more. It fizzled out and I returned home, went to university and never saw him again until your party. Since then I've dated him a few times, and that's it.'

'I see,' Liz said slowly. 'That explains a lot. So are you still seeing him? After all, it's two weeks today since you met—a record for you, Jacy.' Her friend smiled, and at that moment the food arrived.

'He had to go to California—a bit of an emergency— but, yes, I am still in touch.' Jacy's face lit up with a wide grin, her golden eyes sparkling. She couldn't resist teasing her friend, 'The *netsuke* is as good as mine, Liz.' Not that she would take it, even if she *did* win; but she saw no harm in letting Liz sweat a little. 'As for Leo, he called on Monday and he's calling again tonight. And, yes, he will be back soon. Satisfied? Now can we eat!'

'You lucky dog,' was Liz's only comment, and for the rest of the meal they indulged in the usual women's talk.

On leaving the store, Liz reminded Jacy not to forget the races at Cheltenham a week tomorrow.

'What are you trying to do? Turn me into a hardened gambler? First the bet on the *netsuke*, and now a day at the races.' Liz had explained over lunch how Tom's bank had rented a private box at the Cheltenham Gold Cup meeting, corporate-entertainment stuff, and Liz had persuaded Jacy to go as the party was sadly lacking in females.

Liz laughed. 'Take a day off, it's good for you, and if you stick with Leo another two weeks the prize is yours.'

'Oh, I don't know if I could stand the man that long.' Then she spoiled it by giggling. Jacy was still grinning when she returned to the office.

Her humour deserted her when Leo called that night. 'I'm sorry, Jacy, but I won't get back for at least another week.'

'But I thought you said the ship was due to dock tomorrow? Surely after that there's nothing to worry about?' She admired him for taking care of what was just one small part of his vast business empire, but she ached for him to be back. She saw his face in her mind's eye a hundred times a day. His tall, virile body haunted her dreams, and if her voice sounded sulky she couldn't help it.

'Yes, I know, but I hadn't realised that a cousin of my mother's is a passenger on the boat—an elderly lady not in good health, and I've promised my father I will fly out to the island and personally escort the old dear back to Greece. I have to. She is family.'

'You must have a huge family,' Jacy mused, 'if that party at the Ritz was anything to go by.'

'Yes——' his deep voice sank to a throaty drawl '—and over the past week or two I find I keep having this inexplicable urge to add to it.'

Jacy's breath stopped in her throat. Was he saying what she thought he was saying? She didn't dare believe it, but she couldn't stop the hope that blossomed in her heart. She didn't know how to respond and her hand gripped the receiver, her knuckles white with the strain. Was he suggesting a commitment? Then he burst her bubble by adding, 'But I'm fighting it. I picture Tom's twin boys, have a stiff drink, and it's gone. Enough about me. When can I call you again?'

She gave him the address of the hotel she would be staying at in Manchester, and long after she had put the phone down she was still mulling over Leo's surprising admission, and his equally quick retraction. She would be a fool to read more into his words than he meant. He didn't even *like* her, she reminded herself. He actually thought her home was financed by past lovers. It was sex, a chemical attraction, nothing more; and as long as she went into the relationship with her eyes wide open Leo couldn't hurt her.

The next eight days seemed to Jacy to be the longest of her life. Her trip to Manchester was successful. After spending four days going through records and interviews, she had her culprit, and a good laugh... When Leo called her on the Tuesday she finished the case she could not wait to tell him.

'You sound happy without me,' Leo remarked curtly. 'I hope you're behaving yourself.'

'I am.' She couldn't hold back her chuckle. 'You know the case I was working on with the string of hair-care clinics and then the bottling plant? Well, you'll never guess who was setting all the fires.'

'I have no doubt that, with your inherited talent for unearthing the dirt, you will tell me. But isn't the owner the usual culprit?'

'Not in this case. It was a handsome young man who had unfortunately gone prematurely bald. He'd been a customer for three years. It turned out he was so furious that none of the treatments or the hair restorer had worked after he'd spent thousands trying them that he systematically set out to destroy the whole company by burning the clinics down.'

Deep laughter greeted her revelation. 'Ah, Jacy, you're so good for me; I can always depend on you to lift my spirits. Look after yourself. I'll see you at seven on Saturday, if not sooner.'

Unfortunately Jacy could not depend on Leo to lift her spirits, she thought sadly as she replaced the receiver. His derisory crack about her talent for 'unearthing the dirt' left her in no doubt. Leo might be temporarily eager for her body, but his opinion of her as a person was negligible. He was a sophisticated, expert lover, and she wanted him; lying in bed at night, she

couldn't sleep for the physical ache of frustration that
gnawed at her body. But in her heart of hearts she knew
such a hedonistic arrangement as Leo had in mind would
not suit her.

'Come on, Fredsaid. Come on...' Jacy screamed at the
top of her voice. The chestnut with the white blaze, the
jockey wearing the pink and blue colours of an Arab
sheikh, shot past the winning post half a length in front
of its nearest rival. 'I've won, I've won!' Jacy cried in
delight and, turning around from her vantage-point of
the box window, she pushed her way through the crush
of people to where Liz was standing at the sumptuous
buffet. 'Guess what?' She tapped her on the shoulder.
'Guess what?'

'You've won again.' Liz groaned in mock-horror, and
popped a cracker covered in caviar into her mouth.

'By my calculation, a fiver at ten to one means fifty
pounds and my stake back.' Jacy had no idea how
stunning she looked, her beautiful face alight with joy,
her smart cream and black dog-tooth jacket hung open
to reveal a clinging cream silk blouse tied in a cravat
around her neck, not unlike a jockey's tie; but there all
resemblance to the male ended. A wide black leather
belt emphasised her tiny waist and the matching checked
skirt fitted snugly over her hips to end an inch above
her knee. Plain black high-heeled shoes accentuated her
long legs.

'You'll have to tell me your secret, Jacy. That's the
fourth time you've won today, and muggins here has yet
to back a winner.'

Jacy, her golden hair swept back from her face to fall
in a tumbling mass of curls down her back, laughed out
loud at Liz's woebegone expression. 'Just lucky.'

'You know what they say: lucky with money, unlucky
in love,' a deep, dark voice drawled mockingly behind

her head, and Jacy's heart somersaulted in her chest.
Liz melted tactfully into the background. Jacy spun
round and saw the distinguished figure of Leo standing
about a foot away from her. He looked magnificent in
a pale grey business suit, and pristine white silk shirt.
His glittering dark eyes swept her from head to toe and
then he added, 'But if you play your cards right you
could get both.'

'What? How did you...? Why?' The shock of seeing
Leo so unexpectedly made her intelligence desert her.
His hands were warm and strong as they curved around
her upper arms, drawing her closer. She gazed up at him,
speechless, and saw what was in his eyes: he was going
to kiss her. They were in a room full of people. 'Not
here,' she warned.

'You would be insulted if I didn't,' Leo mocked and
his dark head descended, his mouth covering hers.

Her heart pounded against her ribcage. He was right,
damn him! she thought wryly as her body swayed
boneless in his hold. Her skin felt hot; she felt her nipples
tighten, pressed hard against the firm wall of his muscular chest. His tongue invaded her mouth, and she
stopped thinking altogether...

Leo recovered his composure first, and with a self-
satisfied smile, his dark eyes intent on her flushed face,
he said softly, 'You still want me, Jacy, but patience. I
need to see the last race and then I will take you home.'

She should have objected to his arrogant assumption
that she was his for the taking, but her body had already
betrayed her. Fighting to regain her self-control, she
stepped back. 'You never said why you're here,' she
queried. Had he returned to England earlier than expected and checked with her office and followed her?
she imagined happily, very flattered.

'Tom invited me, but I didn't expect to be back in
time. But I got in a couple of hours ago, and as I have

a horse running in the last race I thought I might as well drive down and pick up the trophy personally,' Leo explained with casual arrogance as he turned and took a glass of champagne from a passing waiter.

So much for her over-active imagination, Jacy thought drily, and was glad Leo had not seen the flash of disappointment in her face as he turned back to her, taking a sip from the crystal glass.

'I didn't know you kept racehorses,' she said coolly. 'And aren't you being just a little premature?' One finely arched brow rose mockingly. 'There are seven other horses in the race, Leo.' She was proud of her sophisticated response. Even though her insides were churning with sexual excitement...

'Not at all, Jacy, sweetheart. Haven't you realised yet? I always win.' His dark eyes held hers and she had the oddest feeling there was a warning in his statement, but as he continued talking she dismissed the disturbing thought from her mind, seduced by the deep, rich tone of his voice. 'I had Greek Legend sent over from my racing stables in France specifically for this race. It is one of the best of my string, so take my advice and have a flutter on it.'

She glanced down at the race card in her hand, and sure enough number three, Greek Legend, with the owner's name Kozakis next to it, was there. Some perverse sense of independence made her say, 'I don't know, Leo, I rather fancy Royal Speedmaster.'

'You're joking; what on earth for? It's only won once in two years.'

'Well, this meeting is patronised by the Queen Mother,' she said defensively.

'And that's your reason for picking it?' He threw back his dark head and burst out laughing. 'Jacy, you will never make a gambler. If I were you I would keep your investigative instincts for your career. They won't help you on the race track, but I can if you do as I say.'

'For your information,' she grinned, poking him playfully in the chest, 'I have won a considerable amount of money today.'

Leo put his glass down on the table and took her hand in his. 'OK, please yourself; far be it from me to come between a woman and her intuition,' he drawled cynically, his dark eyes grazing over her smiling face. 'But be warned...' He drew her forward, taking her hand behind her back to hold her hard against his tall frame. 'You won't win.'

His nearness was like a potent force enveloping her. She felt the leashed power in his body; she had never known a man who could affect her as physically as Leo did. The smile left her lips and she stared up into his glittering dark eyes, and inexplicably a shiver of fear slithered down her spine. 'How can you be so sure?' she asked softly, and she saw something dark and dangerous flash in his eyes.

'Because I always do, Jacy...'

CHAPTER SEVEN

JACY, held captive in his hold, her golden eyes trapped by the desire she recognised in Leo's, felt the shiver turn into a tingling sensation down the length of her spine. He was a hard man, all steel, the toughest man she had ever met or was ever likely to. Yet she knew with a deep feminine instinct that Leo was as aware of her as she was of him. The words he spoke were probably true. But they were secondary to the invisible tension that enveloped them.

'And also because I'm a genius,' he opined, his voice harsher, and, as though he resented the tension between them, he released his hold on her.

'And modest with it,' she murmured sarcastically.

'Of course.' The corner of his mouth quirked in the beginnings of a grin and with a slow, salacious study of her feminine curves, neatly displayed by the high-necked blouse and hip-hugging skirt, he added, 'And you are immodest enough for both of us in that outfit.' His arm curved around her waist under her jacket. 'The tie at your throat is begging to be unknotted. How anything so masculine in design can appear so feminine is one of the mysteries of life.'

'Well, we women need some secrets,' she responded with a mock-flirtatious flutter of her long eyelashes, playing his sophisticated game.

'And you, I think, have more than most. Gambling appears to be another one of your vices,' he said hardly.

'Another one? I wasn't aware I had any vices.' *Until I met you*, she wanted to add. Her lust for Leo was her

110

one great weak spot, and inside she died a little. Leo desired her, but it was becoming more and more obvious that his opinion of her as a person had not changed at all.

'If you say so, my sweet. I won't argue; your character or lack of it isn't what I am interested in.' His dark head bent and he pressed a swift, hard kiss on her full lips, and before she could take him up on his comment an announcement over the public address system announced that the horses were going down for the last race.

Suddenly they were besieged by the rest of the party—businessmen demanding from Leo if his horse stood a chance, a rush to place bets, and a hasty scramble for the best view of the track by some, while others were content to watch the race on the television screen provided in the private box. Throughout it all Leo kept Jacy pinned to his side, making it very obvious she was his woman.

For the next half-hour she lived in a mad whirl of excitement. She deliberately squashed any lingering doubts about the wisdom of taking up with Leo again. She only had to look at him to recall the hard potency of his superb male form, and feel the heat curl in her belly. She smiled and laughed, entering wholeheartedly into the various discussions with the ease that long years of working in a high-powered job and travelling extensively to interview and investigate businessmen from the bankrupt to the multi-millionaire had given her.

On a purely practical level, she acknowledged, at eighteen she had been no match for Leo, but now she could confidently move in his sophisticated world with comparative ease, and the thought was oddly comforting, in that they had something in common other than sex. Still, it did not stop her eyes from lingering on his impressive features or her pulse from racing like a gauche teenager's every time he smiled down at her.

Finally the race was off, and she watched along with everyone else as the horses chased around the two-mile four-furlong course. She couldn't repress a groan as hers fell at the fourth jump, but by the final straight she was cheering Greek Legend along with everyone else. Her own stubborn pride had made her stick to her choice, and when Leo's was first past the post she was picked up in his arms and swung around while Leo grinned like an overgrown schoolboy on his first date. When he finally set her back on her feet and she recovered her breath she managed to say, 'Congratulations. But don't say it...'

'I told you so...? As if I would be so cruel...' He laughed, and insisted she join him at the presentation of the trophy in the winners' enclosure.

Leading in the winning horse, standing in the ring with Leo as he accepted the trophy and fat cheque, cameras whirling, and then joining him for a cheerful walk back up to the box for a celebratory toast, Jacy was beguiled into believing he cared.

Liz caught her arm as Leo was accepting the congratulations of Tom and his boss. 'Leo taking you back to London, is he?'

'I——'

'Of course I am, Liz,' Leo cut in briefly before turning back to Tom. 'Thank you, Tom, I'll be in touch.'

'It's customary to ask first,' Jacy muttered, not realising she had spoken out loud.

'Oh-oh, I smell a fight,' Liz quipped. 'Good luck, Leo.' And she was swallowed up by the crowd.

'Why? Are you going to refuse?' Leo queried silkily. 'I was under the impression you had missed me the past couple of weeks, but perhaps I was misled.' His arm tightened around her waist.

'No,' she admitted. Her golden gaze rested helplessly on his bronzed face. What was the point in denying herself or Leo? 'And I did miss you,' she answered honestly.

'I find that hard to believe. You're a very beautiful, very sexy woman. Didn't you feel just a little deprived, waiting for me?' he queried with a cynical smile that did not quite reach the deep brown eyes lingering watchfully on her glowing face.

But Jacy didn't notice his cynicism, or the lack of humour in his smile. She was too hypnotised by the overpowering masculine aura of the man, and with unconscious feline grace she curved her body more snugly into his.

'Well, Jacy?' he demanded. 'No reply, or frightened you might incriminate yourself?'

'Deprived of you,' she drawled languidly. 'But the wait was worth it,' she whispered and felt the rising pressure of his masculine arousal as his hand slid lower to her buttocks and turned her hard against him. She sucked in her breath as fire coursed through her veins. It was as though the rest of the room, the people, had disappeared, and there was only Leo. He filled her mind and her senses to the exclusion of all else.

'Let's get out of here. I can't wait any longer,' Leo growled impatiently, holding her for a long moment, still and rigid against him, as the sexual tension shimmered in the air around them, heavy with need and unspoken desire.

She was unaware of the knowing looks, and the surprised glances, as minutes later Leo, with admirable restraint, made their polite goodbyes and ushered her downstairs and out into the pale evening light. Meekly she followed him across the grass to the car park.

'Get in the car,' he said curtly, opening the door to a long black Jaguar, and then swinging into the driving seat.

The fresh air finally broke through the sensual haze Jacy had been living in for the past few minutes, and rather nervously she pulled the hem of her skirt down to her knees as she sank into the soft leather upholstery of the passenger seat. Was she ready for this? she asked herself.

With a squeal of burning rubber the car shot forward down the entrance drive to the racecourse and out on to the open road towards London. 'It's about two hours' drive to the city; would you like to stop somewhere *en route* for dinner?'

'Not really, I've been munching on caviar, chicken and just about anything else you can name all afternoon. Tom's bank certainly knows how to entertain,' she said conversationally, hoping to defuse the air of electric tension filling the car.

'In that case we'll go to your place; it's slightly nearer,' Leo opined bluntly, casting her a brief sidelong glance, and, as if sensing her growing awareness of their abrupt departure, he dropped one hand from the wheel and gently stroked her thigh through the soft wool of her skirt. 'Your trouble is, you think too much, Jacy. Relax and enjoy; we've waited a long time to be alone together.' His dark voice deepened perceptibly.

She looked across at his starkly etched profile. She could not see the expression in his eyes, but as his long fingers teased towards her inner thigh she swallowed hard, the sexual tension back in full force. Jacy covered his hand with her own. 'My place is fine,' she managed to say. 'But I would like us to get there in one piece, so both hands on the wheel, please.' She tried to lighten the atmosphere, but in the close confines of the car his nearness seemed to affect her breathing and heighten her awareness of him.

'I'll please you; don't doubt it, sweetheart,' he murmured, and squeezed her slender hand for an instant before returning his own to the wheel.

She breathed out shakily. What was she afraid of? Hadn't she decided it was time she grew up? Leo wanted her and, dear heaven, she wanted him. They were friends now. Of a sort, a little voice taunted, and soon to be lovers. She sat up straight in the seat, and with a terrific effort of will managed to ask almost levelly, 'Did you see your aunt safely home all right?'

'Yes.'

'Was it a good trip?' she blundered on, trying to ignore the play of muscles in his thigh as his foot worked the pedals. She raised her eyes to his hands on the wheel— such strong, tanned hands, and she could almost feel them on her naked flesh.

'Yes.' Another blunt reply.

'You're not very talkative,' she prompted huskily.

'We've talked enough over the past few days. What I have in mind now is something else again,' he drawled huskily. 'At the moment my priority is reaching your damn house.' He shot her a quick dark glance, and returned his attention to the road.

Jacy's lips curved in a secret feminine smile. Leo was suffering from the same frustration she was feeling, and the discovery wasn't at all displeasing. She laid her head back against the seat, and, whether it was the champagne or simply the smooth motion of the car, in minutes she was asleep.

'We've arrived, sleepyhead.'

She opened her eyes and for an instant did not know where she was. Leo was leaning over her, his handsome face only inches from her own, and she smiled softly.

Lifting her hand, she stroked his cheek. 'Leo,' she murmured, and his lips covered hers in a deep, drugging kiss.

Minutes later she was standing on the doorstep of her home, and with shaking fingers trying to find the door-key in the bottom of her bag. Leo wasn't helping as, with one arm around her waist, his dark head bent and his firm lips nuzzled provocatively on her neck. She found the key, but had great difficulty trying to put it in the lock, her hand was trembling so much.

'For God's sake, Jacy, give it to me.' And, taking the key from her, he opened the door and propelled her inside.

Automatically she switched on the hall light, and turned back to glance at Leo. Suddenly nervous, all her self-protective instincts coming to the fore, she was about to mouth the obvious cliché, Would you like a coffee? But when her golden eyes met his, for a second she was struck dumb by the flash of barely controlled violence in the depths of his dark eyes.

Dynamic and all male, he projected a raw virility that was almost frightening in its intensity. An involuntary shiver snaked down her spine. Tall and dark, he towered over her; she could sense the unbridled masculine aggression in his still form. 'Leo...' His name a question on her lips, she stepped back.

'No, Jacy,' he gritted. 'Not this time.'

Jacy made a feeble effort to restrain him as he pulled her to him, but they both knew it was only a token gesture. His mouth found hers and in moments all her last-minute doubts had vanished.

She should have been horrified by the savagery of his kiss, but instead her mouth opened and she welcomed the fierce sexual demand apparent in the hard force of his mouth and tongue. His teeth pulled on her lower lip and she swallowed his hot breath with her own. His strong hands stroked up her back and down to her buttocks, hauling her into the hard masculine heat of his taut thighs. Her feet left the floor as he lifted her, better to fit the muscled contours of his superb physique, and then somehow he was carrying her up the narrow stairs, his mouth grazing her cheeks, her throat, urgent and enticing.

Her slender arms wrapped around his broad shoulders. She exulted in his passion and returned it whole-heartedly. This is what the last few weeks had been leading up to; what she had been aching for for the last few hours, and even if she had wanted to she could not have stopped Leo. Her mind might query the wisdom of her response, but her physical being was incapable of denying him anything.

She wasn't aware when or how they reached her bedroom. He lowered her slowly down the long length of him, making her achingly aware of every muscle and sinew in his tall frame, then deliberately stepped back, setting her free. Dazedly she recognised by the landing light slanting through the door her familiar room and narrow bed. Her eyes sought his in the semi-darkness, and she was captivated by the glittering intensity in his black gaze. She lowered her eyes against the fire in his, and watched as he slipped off his jacket and, flinging it and his tie to the floor, unfastened his shirt and dropped it to join the rest on the floor.

'What are you waiting for, Jacy?' he demanded harshly, his voice throbbing with some emotion. 'Or do you want me to do the honours?'

Her heart was pounding like a sledge-hammer, her palms damp, her whole body flushed with heat. She could not tear her eyes away from the thick mat of black hair across his broad chest. Surely he had not looked so good years ago? His presence now surpassed any memory she had ever had of him. She shrugged off her jacket and skirt and then stopped, suddenly shy. Nothing that had happened before could compare with the sheer intensity of her want, her desire for him. She swallowed convulsively, her eyes flicking to his finely chiselled mouth, and then she was in his arms again.

Her lips parted willingly at the intimate insistence of his tongue, and she gave herself up to the incredible sensation his kiss aroused. She never noticed as he pulled the tie at her throat and her blouse fell to the floor; she was lost in examining with tactile delight the breadth and strength of Leo's torso. Then Leo's dark head lowered, trailing down her throat until his mouth covered one aching nipple through the soft silk of her last garment, a brief white silk teddy.

A low groan escaped her; her head fell back over his arm as her body arched wantonly, offering him her breasts. The teddy fell away and she was naked, but she felt no shame. Her small hands slid and clung to his shoulders, then with a will of their own stroked down to claw at the fastening of his trousers.

Leo moaned deep in his throat as her fingers inadvertently scraped over his hard muscled belly. In seconds he was naked and with strong arms he gripped her upper arms, holding her away from him. 'First I want to look at you,' he growled, his dark eyes narrowed to mere slits in the hard contours of his handsome face as he studied her: the high, full breasts, the deep rose nipples, swollen and taut, her narrow waist and the soft feminine flare of her hips. His eyes lingered on the golden crown of curls at the apex of her thighs; his throat worked jerkily. 'God, but you're even more exquisite than I remembered. How the hell do you do it? So innocent on the outside and so...'

Leo stopped on a rasping groan, as Jacy, no longer in control of her own desire, reached out as if in a dream and wound a short, silky chest curl around her index finger and tugged gently.

For Jacy the room turned and she was on the bed, Leo's hard body pinning her to the mattress. Naked, flesh against flesh, she whimpered little erotic sounds of want and almost pain, as Leo, in a frenzy of tumultuous action, fed on her lips, her throat, the curve of her breast. His mouth suckled feverishly on her nipples, first one and then the other, as his strong hands traced the outline of her slender body, his fingers stroking, nipping, teasing, searching out every pulse and pleasure point, and finally, splaying her legs apart, he sank his hard weight between her thighs, his hands biting into her buttocks, lifting her off the bed, as in one savage, demonic thrust he joined his body with hers.

Jacy gasped aloud at the raw, driving urgency of their coupling, and felt a second's pain, a tightness that made her cry out again. Leo, conscious of her action, stopped, and held her for a moment suspended in time, allowing her body to adjust to accept his vital, utterly male possession. Her arms wrapped round his broad back; her fingernails raked down the satin flesh, drawing blood as his mouth covered hers and the fire of his passion seared her innermost being. Her long legs wrapped tightly around his waist and it was the final action that shattered Leo's rigid self-control, as with a tormented cry he tore his mouth from hers, and, burying his head in her throat, he thrust hard and fast, building to a shattering crescendo he was incapable of controlling.

For Jacy the world spun away, her body one pulsating mass of indescribable ecstasy. She heard Leo's hoarse, triumphant cry as his life force exploded into her in a shuddering convulsion that went on and on in a tidal wave of pleasure.

How long they lay locked together, the aftermath of their tempestuous coupling still sending rippling shockwaves through their sweat-slicked bodies, Jacy had no idea. Slowly the real world began to infringe on her consciousness, and the dawning realisation that there was no going back from here. She was once again in Leo's arms, his lover...

This time would be different, she told herself with a soft sigh of satisfaction, and, glorying in his weight above her, she tenderly pressed her open palms to his pounding chest, thrilled at the chaotic beating of his powerful heart. Proof, if proof were needed, that he was as shaken as she by the white heat of their passion.

Leo reared up and looked down at her hot, flushed face. He lifted a hand and stroked the tumbled mass of her hair from her brow. 'I'm sorry if I hurt you, but it's been a long time.'

'For me too,' Jacy admitted, while ruefully recognising that it had probably been a heck of a lot longer for her than Leo, but she was not about to tell him that and upset their new-found relationship. 'And you didn't hurt me,' she added breathlessly, raising a finger to lightly tap his nose. 'But you did get a bit carried away.' She grinned. 'I seem to remember you used to be a very gentle lover.' And he had been. But she realised tonight it had been the fierce, unbridled passion of two equally frustrated adults.

'Gentle? I lost that long ago,' he said cynically, but in an oddly possessive gesture he swept her hair to one side and across the pillow. 'I used to dream of your golden hair splayed across my pillow,' he mused, almost as though he was talking to himself. 'How many blondes? How many nights? The face became...' He stopped abruptly, and in a flurry of Greek he swung off the bed and to his feet.

Jacy stretched languorously on the bed, and rolled over on her side to watch him make for the bathroom, she presumed, but she was wrong. 'What are you doing?' she asked, sitting up on the bed and pulling the cover up over her breasts. It was a stupid question, she knew.

Leo had quickly found his clothes and was pulling them on. 'Leo.' He turned to look at her and a shiver of fear had her clutching the cover between her breasts with both hands.

Wearing only his pants and standing in the middle of the room, he looked every inch the powerful, magnetic tycoon, no trace of his previous lack of control, or any trace of emotion in his hard gaze. A sardonic glint of amusement lit his dark eyes as he answered, 'I'm dressing, Jacy, darling. Surely you've seen a man dress before now.'

'Yes... No...' she stuttered, his endearment grating oddly on a raw nerve. She suddenly realised she had no idea of how to act in the aftermath of their lovemaking. What had she expected? That he would hold her in his arms and declare his eternal love? Well, maybe not that, but at least she had thought he would show he cared. But this stony-faced man standing in her bedroom bore no relationship to the man she had only minutes earlier shared her bed and body with.

'What's wrong, Leo?' she asked quite steadily, fighting back her uncertainty.

'Nothing's wrong, Jacy; if anything you are even better than I remembered,' he drawled silkily, fastening his shirt.

His words should have reassured her; instead they sounded suspiciously like an insult. She eyed him warily, her gaze puzzled and slightly fearful. 'Thank you, I think,' she murmured.

'The pleasure was all mine, Jacy. But you were right about the bed—it is too small. Before you entertain any other man I suggest you invest in a bigger one,' he derided mockingly, and slipped on his jacket.

Before she entertained... She could not believe her ears, and with a sinking heart she studied his shuttered face. 'I never bring men home.'

'In that case I am suitably grateful.'

Jacy recognised the sarcasm, but could find no reason for it. 'Grateful?' she parrotted.

'Yes.' And, slipping his hand in the inside pocket of his jacket, he withdrew a long jeweller's box. 'I did intend to give you this earlier, but in the heat of the moment I forgot.' Walking towards her, he dropped the box in front of her on the bed.

There was something dreadfully wrong; every nerve in her body screamed the warning, but she could not bring herself to believe it. She picked up the box, and glanced questioningly up at Leo, unaware of the pleading light in her golden eyes.

'Here, allow me.' Sitting down, he took the box, snapped it open, and before her startled gaze withdrew an exquisite pearl and diamond pendant in the shape of a heart on a heavy gold chain. Lifting the heavy fall of her hair from her shoulders, he placed it around her neck, and with a quick adjustment settled the jewel between the soft curve of her breasts.

The touch of his fingers against her flesh, the warmth of his breath against her cheek, and she could feel the stirring of renewed arousal. 'It's beautiful, Leo, but you shouldn't have bought me anything.' Maybe she was imagining his coolness, and everything was all right, she told herself, and she stretched out her hand to him, but with an abrupt movement he shrugged her away and once more stood up.

'Rubbish, you deserve it, darling, and I can only apologise for not managing to obtain an antique *netsuke*; I know that is what you prefer.' He walked across the room and stopped with his hand on the door-handle, the light from the open door illuminating his harsh features. 'But you understand pressure of business; I had no time to go hunting in antique shops. My visit to London was only for a month and then, of course, there was my unforeseen trip to America. You know how it is; you're in a high-powered business yourself.'

'How did you know I collect *netsuke*?' she asked, but she was horribly afraid she already knew the answer. Wrapping the cover firmly around her naked body, she slid off the bed and walked towards him, her eyes searching his hard, handsome face. 'I don't remember telling you.'

'You didn't; I overheard you at Liz's party. The picture you drew was very erotic; what was it you said? ''Mr Kozakis will not ask me out, even if I were to strip naked in front of him.'' Wrong, Jacy.' He shook his dark head; a slow, sensuous smile curved his hard mouth. 'You grossly underestimate yourself, my dear. I determined to have you the minute I set eyes on you again. As for your bet with Liz, I'm afraid you're going to be disappointed. I'm leaving London tomorrow, and I don't know when I will be back.'

Jacy realised in stricken apprehension that Leo had known about the bet all along. Surely he couldn't believe that was the reason she'd gone out with him? She lifted her free hand and placed it on his shirt front. 'You've got it all wrong, Leo.' If she explained...

With a dismissive gesture he flicked her hand from his shirt front. 'No, I was right about you the first time.' He slashed her a scornful glance, his mouth compressed in a tight line. 'Then it was to help your career, and now for an ornament.'

She could not speak; her tongue was glued to the dry roof of her mouth as she stared at him in shocked horror. Leo really thought so badly of her...

'A word of advice, Jacy...' And with one hand he reached out and tore the cover from her fingers so she was left standing naked before him. His dark eyes roamed over her in blatant cynical appraisal. 'You're a beautiful woman, but certainly no saleswoman. You sell yourself far too cheap, and, as for gambling, let this be a lesson to you—forget it. Your face is far too expressive; you will never make a poker player,' he derided mockingly.

Jacy was incapable of movement, stunned by his cutting words and the dawning realisation that their lovemaking had meant less than nothing to him.

Tanned fingers closed around her wrist. He jerked her up against his hard body. 'Mute, always the silent act when you're found out. But God! I still fancy you.' Her golden eyes widened fearfully as Leo's fingers pushed up her chin, devilish amusement burning in his gaze. 'Don't worry, not again tonight; I haven't time.'

The stark assurance in his deep-timbred drawl held her mesmerised, but as the full import of his words sunk in she shivered, suddenly aware of her nakedness and the ice creeping through her veins.

'I'll give you a call the next time I'm in London.' With an icy smile his fingers fell from her chin and his hand left her wrist. 'Get back to bed; you'll catch cold.' And, picking the cover from the floor in an oddly gentle gesture, he wrapped it around her shoulders. 'I'll let myself out.'

He left her standing there. How long Jacy stood looking vacantly at the open bedroom door she had no idea; she was listening intently to the loud hammering of her heart. Why hadn't it stopped? A broken heart should stop, she thought fuzzily, and then like an old woman she staggered over to the bed and lay down on it, pulling the cover firmly around her like a shroud. She curled up in a little ball and willed the pain to go away as tears fell unchecked from her pain-hazed eyes.

Jacy awoke slowly, a niggling warning teasing her consciousness. She struggled up into a sitting position and rubbed the sleep from her eyes with her soft hands, and then it hit her...

She doubled over in pain, her stomach somersaulting, nausea clawing at her throat. She dragged herself to the bathroom and was physically sick. She lifted her head and, grasping the wash-basin, ran the cold water tap, splashing her face over and over again. Finally she straightened and stared at her reflection in the mirror over the wash-basin. The laughing, glowing woman of yesterday had vanished and in her place stood a poor replica. Her eyes were red, and her colour ashen. Between her full breasts lay the pearl and diamond heart. With slow deliberation she loosened the clasp and held it in the palm of her hand. Her payment for sex. She let it drop through her shaking fingers to the floor.

Leo Kozakis, her nemesis. Was she never going to learn? she asked herself bitterly. He had made love to her and walked out to teach her a lesson! It would be laughable if it didn't hurt so much, but she had only herself to blame. How simply she had fallen into his arms, just as she had ten years ago. Only this time it was a hundred times worse. At least at eighteen she had been in love with him and had believed Leo loved her. Last night she had been under no such illusion. She had been perfectly well aware of Leo's reputation, but had justified her own surrender on the strength of a few conversations with the man and a foolishly held belief that, with age and maturity, this time with Leo would be different. She groaned out loud; she had reduced her expectations of love and marriage in favour of a more realistic adult relationship, only to find herself used once more.

Well, that was it! Never again, she vowed, and walked back into her bedroom and forced herself to follow her usual morning ritual. Dressing in a pair of old, well washed jeans and a soft blue cashmere sweater, she applied a minimum of make-up to her pale face, but could do nothing to disguise the dark circles under her eyes,

or the haunted look she was unable to hide. Thank God
she had taken the Thursday and Friday off work in lieu
of working last weekend. There was no way she could
have gone to the office today.

She glanced at the rumpled bed; a brief image of
herself and Leo, naked, entwined in the throes of passion,
flashed vividly through her mind. Clenching her teeth,
she marched out of the room. Passing the door to the
main bedroom, she hesitated and, pushing it open,
walked in. No memories of Leo here, only of her father.

A deep sigh escaped her. Her father, bless him, had
returned to England as the editor of a serious British
newspaper after the death of her mother, and bought
the house, quite happily making a home for Jacy as well.
She crossed to the wide bed and sat down. It was a
pleasant room, decorated in shades of beige and brown,
and very reminiscent of her father. Unbidden, she recalled her father's words when she had once asked him
if he was going to marry again. At the time he had been
going out with a very attractive lady reporter, and Jacy
had had visions of having to move out to make room
for his new wife.

'Jacy, my pet, whatever advice your mother gave you
about sex, the only thing you need to remember is an
old Scottish saying, "A man will never buy the bottle if
he can drink of the whisky free"'.' And then he'd laughed.

She should have remembered his advice, she thought,
rising to her feet and walking slowly to the door. All
men were basically the same. Leo, even her own father...
She had loved him dearly and after he'd died she had
never bothered changing her bedroom for his much larger
one. Perhaps now it was time she did. She knew in her
heart she would never again sleep happily in the bed she
had shared with Leo. In a flurry of activity—anything
to stop herself thinking—she transferred all her be-
longings to the master bedroom.

Finally by mid-afternoon she collapsed on the sofa in her living-room, a cup of coffee and a plate of sandwiches which she had no desire to eat on the table in front of her. She drank the coffee and laid her head back against the soft cushions. It was no good; she could not hold back the memories of yesterday any longer, however hard she tried.

The events of the evening ran through her head like a recurring nightmare. Leo had known about the bet all along, from the very night she had made it with Liz, and yet the devious swine had never mentioned it. Not until last night after he had finally got her into bed. Then he had cold-bloodedly thrown it in her face, and added a chilling denouncement of her character. To top it all he had then had the audacity, after once again just about calling her a whore, to turn around and say he'd call...

With hindsight she could see there had been plenty of clues. More than once she had wondered if he knew about the bet, but after he'd gone to America, and their long conversations, she had put it out of her mind. But Leo quite obviously hadn't. He had delighted in throwing it in her face.

She cringed with shame as she recalled the frenzied lovemaking. He had wanted her; that was some consolation, she tried to tell herself, but it was poor comfort when she considered how the evening had ended. He had used her and she had let him. She was an astute businesswoman, but she might as well admit that in the male-female relationship stakes she was a non-starter and resign herself to the fact. Her body ached for the satisfaction only Leo could provide, but with a steely determination she resolved to put him out of her mind for good. She had done it once and she could do it again, she vowed silently.

The phone rang and she reluctantly answered it.

'Hi, Jacy, are you alone?' Liz's happy voice queried.

'Yes,' Jacy said flatly.

'Do I discern a lovers' tiff so soon?'

'No lover and no tiff.'

'Don't tell me you've blown it, Jacy. You only had to keep in with Leo until next Tuesday and the *netsuke* was yours.'

'As I have no intention of ever seeing Leo Kozakis again, tell me when you want me to baby-sit.' And for the first time in her long friendship with Liz she lied. 'Sorry, Liz, someone at the door, I must go. Bye.'

CHAPTER EIGHT

JACY had only delayed the inevitable as at four in the afternoon a knock on the door heralded the arrival of Liz.

'You sounded funny earlier and I was coming up to town to meet Tom, so I've told him to pick me up here. I thought I'd call and see how you are. The speed Leo carried you off yesterday was unbelievable. He was eating you with his eyes. So come on, what went wrong?'

'Nothing. We returned here. Leo had coffee. We talked and he left.' Jacy did not tell lies easily, but even for Liz, her best friend, she could not bare her soul. It still hurt too much...

'Washed out complexion, red-rimmed eyes, and you're not going to tell me, hmm?' Liz queried, sitting down in the wing-backed chair, her pixie face full of compassion. 'It might help to talk, and I'm a great listener.'

A wry smile brightened Jacy's face for a second. 'You never give up, Liz, but this time I'm afraid you'll have to. Suffice it to say you were perfectly correct when you warned me about Leo after Tom's birthday party. He is too much the cynical sophisticate for me. So now can we change the subject? Please...'

Liz regarded her candidly. 'Are you going to be OK?' she queried. 'Or shall I get Tom to punch Leo out for you...? No, perhaps that's not such a good idea. Tom is hoping to clinch Leo's considerable business for the bank and end up chairman. Breaking the bloke's nose might not enhance his prospects.'

Jacy laughed at that, and until Tom arrived the conversation carefully avoided any mention of Leo.

It was only after they had left and the silence of her home began to press in on her that Jacy realised sadly just how much subconsciously she had been hoping this time with Leo would be different. The house had never seemed so empty before, and she had never felt so alone. Much to her own self-disgust she found herself praying for the telephone to ring.

Rubbish, pull yourself together, girl! There was life after Leo before, and there would be again, she told herself firmly, and of course this time she didn't love Leo! That had ended years ago. She could not deny the physical attraction between them. Last night it had reached breaking-point. A temporary madness, she assured herself, but as she ascended the stairs to her changed bedroom she could not help recalling how only a few hours ago she had been carried tenderly up the same stairs in the arms of her lover.

She shuddered, her blood turning to iced water in her veins. It had been hard enough admitting her mistake the first time, but at least she had the excuse of extreme youth and naïveté. This time it was a much greater humiliation. She was a mature woman and the blow to her own self-respect, self-image, doubly hard to endure.

Almost three weeks later Jacy sat curled up on the sofa in her 'Save the Whale' night-shirt, a plate of raw mushrooms and a huge strawberry cream cake on the table in front of her, with a pot of tea, and the daily paper open at 'What's on TV'.

Yes, she congratulated herself quietly, the hurt was easing. Leo hadn't called, but then she hadn't expected him to. He hadn't lied to her; he had suggested a brief affair, and that was all it had been. She couldn't really blame Leo. Anger at Barbara's treatment had encouraged her to make the stupid bet. How could she expect a proud man like Leo Kozakis to react when he found out other than to take delight in turning the tables on her? He had told her himself he always won. Now she knew it was true... Leo had shown himself in his true light. His relationships with women were, and always would be, shallow. He had made love to Jacy because he wanted to teach her a lesson, while she had secretly nursed the hope that their relationship might develop into something more. In her business life she was a tough go-getter, but she could never handle the kind of meaningless, sophisticated relationships Leo Kozakis indulged in. How she had fooled herself otherwise on the strength of a few telephone calls she couldn't bear to contemplate.

Instead she had immersed herself in her work, and she was not without friends. Next weekend was Easter and she was spending it looking after the twins, while Liz and Tom went to Paris. More immediate, she loved opera, and tomorrow, Friday, Simon was taking her to Covent Garden to hear Placido Domingo in *Tosca*.

She picked up a mushroom and popped it into her mouth before turning her attention to the paper. She was trying to decide between *Roseanne* and the ten o'clock news when the telephone rang. Damn! Who could it be at this time of night? she wondered and, strolling into the hall, unsuspecting, picked up the receiver.

The breath wooshed out of her body in one long gasp of amazement. Leo...

'I'm back in London for a while; I saw Tom yesterday and he tells me you're still free. Sorry I couldn't get in touch sooner. I don't usually kiss and run, but business... You know how it is.'

The cool cheek of the man took her breath away. But with remarkable self-control she managed to respond with biting sarcasm, 'Think nothing of it. I haven't...'

And read what you like into that, she muttered under her breath.

'Good, I knew you would understand. So how about coming to Covent Garden tomorrow evening, the opera, with——?'

Jacy cut in, 'Placido Domingo. I know, I have a ticket; I'm going with Simon.' Nothing in her life had ever given her so much satisfaction, she thought elatedly, delighted at the coincidence that had enabled her to turn Leo down flat.

'The red-headed guy at the party.' The dark voice cracked like broken glass.

'Yes. But thank you for thinking of me.' In a voice sickly sweet, leaving him in no doubt that she was sure the opposite was true, she added, 'I hope you enjoy it; I'm sure I shall.'

'No doubt I will; he's a marvellous singer,' Leo responded smoothly, sounding not in the least put out by her refusal. But the deep, rich sound of his voice reawakened all the hurt and longing Jacy had been so desperately trying to suppress, and when he ended with, 'Goodbye, I'll see you around,' she had to bite her tongue to stop herself asking when.

She ate the plate of mushrooms and the cake, washing it down with cold tea. She had saved her pride by turning him down, but a tiny devil whispered in her head that Leo hadn't been very insistent. He could have asked her out another night... Why did he have to ring now? Damn him! Just when she had begun to get her life back on an even keel. Because he was a sadist; he got his kicks out of stringing women along. The answer was obvious, she thought morosely.

Sitting in the front stalls with Simon beside her the next night, even the enormous talent of Placido Domingo could not shake off her dread of bumping into Leo.

It happened in the interval. Simon had managed to secure them two glasses of wine, and after a sip or two she was finally beginning to relax. Simon lounged tall and elegant against the wall and Jacy stood in front of him. Teasingly she said, 'What a waste to womankind, Simon; you really do look incredibly attractive.' And he did, along the lines of a male model, impeccably dressed in a fashionable dinner suit.

'I know, darling, but right now I have a more pressing problem than my sexual predilections. A certain dark Greek is standing across the room and if looks could kill I'd be dead.'

Jacy's hand trembled, spilling a little of the wine. She breathed in deeply and, resisting the urge to turn around, she held her head high, her eyes going to the mirror on the wall beside Simon, reflecting the room behind her. Leo, clad in a perfectly fitting conventional black dinner suit, the plain white silk evening shirt in stark contrast to his swarthy complexion, looked absolutely devastating. He was standing with his arm around Thelma, but his glittering dark eyes were fixed firmly on Jacy. Her stomach felt as though it were on a roller-coaster ride, while her heart pounded against her ribcage until she was sure everyone must hear it. Her throat went dry and she could not tear her eyes away from Leo.

His firm mouth twisted in a polite social smile as he mockingly saluted her with the glass in his free hand.

She couldn't pretend she had not seen him, and stiffly she raised her own glass in greeting, then was struck with a wave of jealousy so intense that she clenched the stem of her wine glass till her knuckles turned white with the strain, as Leo lowered his dark head to his companion and whatever he said had the other woman smiling up at him in adoration.

Jacy wanted to scream bitchily, 'You weren't his first choice,' and a treacherous feeling of regret flooded her mind. It could so easily have been her with Leo tonight, if her stupid pride had not got in the way. Taking a hasty swallow of her drink, she looked away. She knew she wasn't being fair to Thelma. The woman was really quite pleasant, a very attractive blonde and an excellent interior designer. But Jacy had no doubt that the designs the other woman had on Leo had nothing to do with furniture. Telling herself not to be so stupid, she breathed a sigh of relief as the bell rang for the next act.

Once more in the auditorium, she was determined to enjoy the second half of the performance. But it was not that easy. A thousand unanswered questions swirled around her troubled mind. Had she been too precipitate in refusing Leo's invitation? Who was she kidding? She meant nothing to the man. Surely seeing him with Thelma at his side had taught her that much. A blonde—any blonde—would do for Leo. Jacy had too much pride, too much self-respect, to be any man's plaything.

'Aunty Jacy, Aunty Jacy,' two young voices chorused in unison. 'It's morning . . .'

Opening one eye, Jacy glared at the bedside clock. Six a.m. She groaned and turned over just as the terrible twins arrived with a thump on top of the bed. The reverberations ricocheted through her body, and stopped in her stomach.

'Yes, OK.' She hauled herself up to a sitting position and eyed the two pyjama-clad little bodies balefully, before gingerly swinging her long legs over the side of the bed. Then it happened: nausea rose up in an overwhelming surge; she could taste the bile in her throat as she made a headlong dash for the bathroom.

Five minutes later, wearily lifting her head from the toilet bowl, she swivelled around and sat on the tiled floor, her face on a level with two angelic-looking blond-haired angels, only the angels sported identical worried frowns.

'Are you sick every day, Aunty Jacy?' Tomas, the older by one minute, asked seriously.

'Apparently,' she murmured, getting to her feet. 'But it's nothing to worry about,' she reassured them, and wished she could reassure herself so easily. The past few days had been hell. She adored Tomas and Jethro, and when she had arrived on Thursday to take care of them for the weekend she had firmly waved Liz and Tom off, prepared to spend a pleasant Easter weekend in the comfort of their luxurious house. But it hadn't turned out like that. Friday morning had seen her waking up sick for the fourth day running, and she knew she could no longer pretend it was something she had eaten. The same thing had happened on Saturday, and now this morning. She could fool herself no longer. A brief calculation in her head confirmed her suspicion. She was two weeks overdue. She couldn't believe her own stupidity...

Luckily, with the twins to look after, she did not have time to brood over her problem, as they occupied every minute of the day. Speedily she washed and dressed, then performed the same service for the boys, amid much giggling and horseplay. Half an hour later, with breakfast prepared, she sat down with her first cup of tea of the day, and a slice of dry toast. She could not face coffee— hadn't been able to for the past week... A warning she had chosen to ignore...

'Don't put your toasted soldiers in your ears, Tomas; they are meant to dip in your egg,' she said bluntly.

'I'm Dr Spock.'

'Dr Spock had pointy ears, not toast sticking out of them,' she said matter-of-factly, adding, 'Now what are we going to do today?'

'Sunday school this morning, Sunday school this morning,' both boys started to chant.

Jacy breathed an inward sigh of relief. She could drive them to the village church for ten o'clock and have a couple of hours to herself before she had to pick them up again at twelve.

It had not been a very productive break, she thought with wry self-mockery as once more she let herself out of the Tudor house and locked the oak door behind her. She had spent most of it chewing her thumbnail and cursing Leo Kozakis. Still, she might be wrong, she told herself, pulling the soft blue cashmere sweater rather self-consciously down over her jeans-clad behind. Was she already subconsciously trying to hide an imaginary bump? Striding across to her car, she inserted the key in the lock, and then hesitated. Lifting her head, she looked down the drive to see another car speeding up. Who could it be? Tom and Liz weren't due back until tomorrow. She waited and as it drew closer, her golden eyes widened to their fullest extent in shocked horror.

The car stopped two feet from her own, and with a rising sense of helplessness she watched as the driver's door opened and out stepped Leo.

'What the hell are you doing here?' she demanded peremptorily, more in self-defence than any real anger. She was too fragile this morning to deal with Leo Kozakis.

One dark eyebrow arched in silent query. 'Is it any business of yours?'

'I'm in charge,' she said sullenly. He was too arrogant, too thoroughly male, she thought with an overwhelming sense of inadequacy. Her pulse was racing and she could do nothing about the nervous fluttering in her stomach.

Leo, casually dressed in a thick cream Aran-styled sweater teamed with designer jeans, the lighter patches sexily outlining the points of tension in the denim, covered the distance between them in a few lithe strides.

'What of?' He glanced derisively around the obviously empty garden, then back to Jacy. 'You sound like a two-bit general who's lost his troops,' he drawled with mocking amusement as he stopped a hand's breadth away.

'I am not interested in your opinion, and if you're looking for Tom and Liz they're away. I'm taking care of the twins.'

'And who is taking care of you?' Leo demanded cynically. 'The red-headed pretty boy?'

'Certainly not,' she snapped, instantly on the defensive. He was too near; the spicy scent of his cologne mingled with the fresh spring air was having a disastrous effect on her breathing. Then to her astonishment Leo suddenly smiled, a breathtaking, face-splitting grin that deepened the slight laughter lines around his sparkling brown eyes and took years off his age.

'I'm glad to hear it, Jacy.' And for a ridiculous moment she thought she saw a flicker of relief in his expression and wondered if he had been jealous of her friendship with Simon, but quickly dismissed the thought as he continued smoothly, 'I know Tom and Liz are away for the weekend, but I promised the boys I would bring them an Easter egg each. So where are they?'

She wanted to ignore him, leap in her car and drive off. He was much too dangerous to her emotional well-being. But he made the request sound so natural that she had no choice but to tell him. 'I'm just going to collect them from Sunday school.'

'Great, we'll take my car; there's more room.' And before she could object Jacy found herself in the front seat of the gleaming Jaguar, as near to the door as she could get, and reluctantly giving Leo directions to the village church.

For a while the only sound was the swish of tyres on tarmac. Jacy determinedly looked out of the side window, keeping her face averted from Leo, but she was achingly aware of every move he made.

'So how are you managing as a surrogate mother?' His deep voice drawled seductively along her overstrung nerves, and the word 'mother' gave her a sinking feeling in her already upset stomach. She said nothing.

'Are the twins running you ragged? You look a bit washed out.'

'I'm fine,' she snapped. So what if he did think she looked a mess? It didn't matter to her. But if he ever found out what was the matter with her, her life would not be her own, she recognised instinctively. Then, frightened she had been too emphatic, she tagged on, 'I love the boys, I can manage perfectly.'

'I wasn't suggesting you couldn't, Jacy,' he said, quietly stopping the car at the entrance to the church. Turning sideways, he studied her huddled form in the corner of the seat. He stretched out a hand and flipped the end of her long blonde hair over her shoulder.

She knew it looked a mess, but this morning she had scraped it back in a ponytail with an elastic band simply for ease. The touch of his hand made the hairs on the back of her neck prickle in alarm, and her hand grasped the door-handle, ready to bolt...

'Still the mute defence, hmm?' he prompted, his hand curved around her shoulder, preventing her exit, quite deliberately allowing the tension to build until finally Jacy could stand no more; she had to look at him.

His dark eyes, strangely intense, held hers and for a long moment something inexplicable passed between them, an emotion so strong that Jacy shivered in fear. Her eyes fell to his mouth; the firm, sensual lips were parted slightly, and she knew if he made a move to kiss her she would not be able to resist. She had refused to go out with him, but only over the telephone, and soberly she realised face to face she had no defence against him. But his next words broke the tenuous thread that held them together.

'Would it be so hard for you to behave as a normal human being for the next couple of hours?' he demanded bitingly, his dark eyes never leaving her pale face. 'I have no desire to upset the children, but if you insist on trying to ignore me or keep a foot of space between us the boys are bound to notice.'

He wasn't interested in her. When was she going to get it in her thick head...? It was the boys he was worried about, and he was right, she knew. He was here to see the twins, and at that moment two voices could be heard screaming in delight at the sight of the long black car.

Opening the door, Leo prompted, 'Well, Jacy— friends?'

'Yes, all right.' She slid out of the passenger seat and greeted the twins.

For the next few hours Jacy was treated to a totally different Leo Kozakis. The ruthless businessman was replaced by a laughing friend who thought nothing of driving to the outskirts of London to lunch in the nearest hamburger restaurant. They returned home to a frantic football game on the front lawn, with a wild disregard for Liz's recently planted flowerbeds, and by six in the evening two bathed, shiny-faced boys lay comfortably on the floor in the elegant drawing-room, a tousled Leo sprawled out beside them while they attempted to build a castle with Lego.

Jacy, stretched out on the sofa, was pretending to read the Sunday paper, but her gaze kept straying to the three on the floor, or more particularly to the man, and remembering the last time she had seen him lying down; then he had been naked and in her bed, his handsome face taut with passion...

'What's wrong? Have I a smut on my nose or something?'

With a guilty start the paper fell from her hands as Leo caught her staring at him. How could she tell him what she had been thinking? 'No, no, nothing like that,' she blurted. 'I was just thinking how good you are with children.'

With the speed and grace of some sleek jungle cat he rose to his feet and came towards her.

'I like kids, and I'm very good with my nephew and nieces, I'll have you know,' he offered, grinning smugly.

'You just don't like how you have to get them?' she said, thinking of his aversion to marriage and his host of casual relationships.

A roar of laughter greeted her comment. 'You couldn't be more wrong, sweetheart.' Collapsing on the sofa beside her, he flung his arm around her shoulder, and, his breath like a summer breeze against the soft curve of her cheek, whispered huskily, 'I love how one has to get children; I couldn't do without it. Shall I show you later?' Then he leant back, still chuckling.

Jacy turned a fiery red with embarrassment. 'I didn't mean that... I meant getting married,' she corrected him furiously.

'True, I have always avoided that particular trap, but——' Whatever Leo might have added was forestalled by the boys.

'Can we have some more of our chocolate egg?' Jethro asked, pulling on Jacy's arm, while his twin was pulling on Leo's arm, demanding another game.

Relieved at the distraction, Jacy eyed her two little charges' flushed faces and tired eyes. 'You have both had enough for one day.' They had been delighted with the huge chocolate eggs Leo had presented them with and had eaten almost half already. 'And Leo has to go now, so how about we see him off, and then bed and a story, hmm?'

'But I want Leo to stay, and I want some more chocolate,' Jethro demanded fractiously.

'Sorry, darling, but it will make you sick; you'll be ill and you wouldn't like that.' She tried to placate the little boy.

'I don't mind,' he said staunchly. 'You're sick every day, Aunty Jacy, and you're all right.'

The blood drained from her face, and for a moment she was speechless. She didn't dare look at Leo; instead, finding her voice, she said, 'Yes, OK, you can have some chocolate, and then bed.' She half stood up, but a large hand around her wrist forced her back down on the sofa. She shot a furious glance at Leo, but his attention was fixed on Jethro and Tomas.

'Has your aunty Jacy been making herself sick with chocolate?' he asked the twins with a grin.

Jacy burnt with humiliation as the boys delighted in giving Leo graphic details of her morning stints with her head in the toilet bowl, ending with the information that after her tea and toast she was fine.

His dark eyes narrowed to slits in the harsh contours of his handsome face as he flashed her a look of such glittering hatred that she flinched as though he had struck her; his fingers dug into the flesh of her shoulder through her sweater. Then abruptly he set her free, as though just to touch her was a contamination.

How she got through the next hour she didn't know. One look at Leo's hard face and she knew her hints that he should leave were pointless. He had guessed she was pregnant . . . and was furiously angry, though he hid it well with the cheerful face he showed the children.

Finally she could delay the confrontation no longer. The boys were in bed and asleep, and with Leo at her

back, following her out of the room, she walked down
the stairs to the drawing-room.

'I need a drink.' Leo crossed to the drinks trolley and
poured himself a large Scotch. 'I won't offer you one.
In your condition I believe it is unwise.' His hard mouth
twisted in a mockery of a smile.

'I have no idea what you're talking about. I'm perfectly all right, and I think it's time you left.' Her legs
were trembling and it took all her will-power to stand
in front of him and try to bluff it out in a last desperate
attempt to deny the inevitable, but it was no good. Leo
slammed his glass down on the trolley and, reaching out,
grabbed her wrist.

'Don't lie to me, Jacy. You're pregnant, aren't you?'

'What the hell has it got to do with you?' She knew
as soon as the words left her mouth that she had made
a mistake. Leo went white about the mouth, his features
settling into a hard, impenetrable mask that filled her
with fear.

'Everything, if it is mine,' he announced in a icy, im-
personal tone. 'And don't try to fool me, Jacy. I will
insist on tests to make sure. You're not sticking me with
that red-headed wimp's offspring.'

She couldn't help it; she started to laugh. It was ironic.
She had been terrified he would find out, and he was
equally terrified in case it was his child. He had said he
didn't want to be trapped, and now, with his insistence
on tests, he would trap himself. It would be hilarious if
it weren't so sad.

'Stop it, Jacy.' His curt command, the pressure of his
fingers on her arm, silenced her laughter.

She sobered instantly. 'It's all right, Leo. I haven't
been to a doctor. It's not certain I'm pregnant; you have
nothing to fear. Even if I am there will be no tests,' she
declared scornfully. He had shown his true colours; he
was a bastard, but then she had always known that, she

thought with rising fury. She didn't notice the flash of
enlightenment in his dark eyes, or the fact she had given
herself away by her declaration; she was too enraged.
Ten years ago she would have been incapable of standing
up to Leo, but not any more.

'I am perfectly capable of taking care of everything
myself. I may not be wealthy according to the law of the
great Leo Kozakis, but I'm not a pauper. I have my own
house.'

'And we both know how you got it; you're hardly
likely to be able to continue with that particular moon-
shine activity.'

His sneering condemnation served to fuel her anger.
'That crude assumption was about what I would expect
from a rat like you. But you're wrong: my father left
me the house.' She was too furious to notice the quick
flash of shocked relief in his expression. 'I won't be
pregnant forever; I have a good career. I don't need a
man, and certainly not you.' Lunging back, she was free
and, swinging on her heel, she would have stormed out.
She couldn't bear to look at him...

A strong hand spun her back around, his fingers biting
into her narrow shoulderblade. Dark eyes glittered down
at her in barely controlled fury. 'You bitch. It is mine
and you had no intention of telling me.'

'Get your hands off me,' she ordered, her anger
wavering as she collided for a brief moment with his
hard body. She jerked back as though hit by lightning,
an odd breathlessness making her breasts heave. His arm
snaked around her waist; deliberately ignoring her
command, he increased his hold on her. 'Leo, let go of
me.' But a constriction in her throat made the sentence
sound like a husky plea, instead of the adamant demand
she had intended.

Dark colour swept up over his high cheekbones, and
a flash of demonic rage lit his glittering gaze. 'You would

abort my child, and return to your career without a
qualm.'

Her eyes widened to their fullest extent as she stared
at him in horror. That was not what she had meant.
How could he so misjudge her? He really did not know
her at all if he could imagine for a second that she would
abort her unborn child. Her mouth worked, but no
words came out...

'No denial, Jacy!'

His eyes hardened until they resembled polished jet,
then he drew her even closer until her breasts pressed
against his broad chest. Slowly his hand at her shoulder
slid to hold the nape of her neck, while his other hand
moved down the base of her spine, moulding her so close
that the pressure of his powerful thighs was almost a
pain.

'You don't need a man, do you?' The query was silky-
soft, but she sensed his rage was held by the slenderest
of threads. 'Liar.' And with a deadly intent he lowered
his head and took her mouth in a savage, bitter kiss that,
although she recognised it was an insult, slowly drained
all the resistance from her body.

His mouth gentled on hers, and her arms slid around
his broad shoulders; her fingers dug into the soft wool
of his sweater, while her lips parted helplessly beneath
his. She melted into the hard heat of his long body, the
blood flowing through her veins, the heavy thudding of
her heart deafening her to everything but the exquisite
taste and touch of Leo.

Suddenly, with an angry oath, he flung her from him,
she almost fell; only Leo's quick reaction saved her, as
he once more caught her arm. She was completely disorientated, still under the spell of his embrace, until her
eyes focused on his face, and she felt as though someone
had thrown a bucket of iced water over her.

His lips twisted in a hard, contemptuous smile. 'You want me; you can't help yourself.' And with that knowledge he appeared to have regained control of his temper. Leading her to the sofa, he pushed her trembling body down. 'Sit down before you fall down, and from now on you are going to do as I tell you... understand?'

He towered over her, tall and indomitable. 'I'm not...' she gasped.

'You and I are going to be married as soon as possible.'

A brittle laugh escaped her. 'You're mad. I'm not marrying you. You said yourself marriage is a trap, and you are not the only one who has no desire to fall into it.'

A dark brow lifted sardonically. 'Oh, I think you will.' Coming down beside her, he gathered her into his arms.

'Sex is no solution,' she managed to get out before his lips closed over hers once more.

Her head fell back against the cushions and her mouth opened instinctively for his. His fingers pulled the band from her hair and wound into the tangled curls. His other hand edged beneath her wool sweater, easing it up, her lacy bra along with it, until his hand was cupping her breast, his long fingers stroking her rosy nipple into instant arousal, while his tongue searched the dark, moist hollow of her mouth to devastating effect. She tried to tell herself he was deliberately seducing her, but his onslaught was too practised, too intense. Before she knew it she was lying full-length on the sofa, her sweater pushed up under her armpits, his hard body over her, as his hands continued their tormenting, wandering over her breasts, the firm swell of her hips, and down her long legs, encased in clinging denim, in confident knowledge of her helpless arousal.

He seduced her utterly. It had been too many weeks since she had felt his touch, and her body writhed against him in aching need.

Abruptly he released her love-swollen lips and lifted his dark head. 'You want me; you can't deny it. I could take you now.' His fingers trailed teasingly over her turgid breasts. 'You will marry me next weekend. Our child will have two parents, and we...we will have this,' he growled, his head once more lowering, but this time to nip teasingly at her breast.

Jacy could barely breathe, her nipples tight, engorged with her surging blood. An ache was arrowing from where Leo's hand covered her groin through every nerve and sinew in her body.

'Say yes...' His mouth whispered the words against her throat. 'You know you want to.' And, raising his head, his derisory gaze lingered on her swollen, pouting lips.

That was the terrible part, she thought in self-hatred. Leo was right, and he knew it. He drove her crazy—he always had and probably always would—but that was no basis for a marriage. 'Anyway, I may not even be pregnant,' she stalled.

'How late are you?'

'Two weeks,' she mumbled, and, glancing warily up at him, she noted the dull flush of passion along his cheekbones. It was a two-way street, she realised, this explosion of the senses whenever they touched.

'Well, then, I'll make arrangements for you to see the doctor on Tuesday and we will be married next Saturday.' His fingers trailed seductively over the soft, creamy mound of her breast, and she couldn't think straight.

'But we don't love each other,' she objected.

'Love is a vastly overrated emotion. What we have is much better.' His fingers plucked at her breast and he chuckled as her body instinctively arched beneath him. 'You're the most responsive woman I have ever bedded, the chemistry is perfect between us, you're pregnant with my child... Many a marriage started with less.'

'No, I won't.' She tried to push him away, the thought of all his other women cooling her over-heated emotions immediately. 'There are other solutions.' He could have visiting rights or something, she thought feebly. She just wasn't cut out for his kind of open-ended commitment, and sadly she recognised it.

'Well, you're not aborting my child.' He swore furiously and hauled her upright and in a deft movement had her sweater back down where it belonged. 'You haven't got a choice.' His jawline hardened. 'Liz and Tom are your friends. He has a glittering career before him, possibly chairman of the bank, but only with my contract under his belt. Do I make myself clear?'

'You ruthless bastard,' she swore unsteadily.

'Maybe.' His hard, dark eyes held hers with cruel mockery. 'But I'll make damn sure my child is not...'

CHAPTER NINE

LEO and Jacy were flying direct to Corfu; Leo's parents had insisted on it. His father, unable to fly because of recent heart surgery, had not been able to attend the simple civil marriage ceremony that morning in London. Instead, Leo had informed Jacy that a large family party had been planned for the evening at the Kozakis villa.

'They know the circumstances of our marriage and it will be easier for you to meet them all at once and get all the ribald comments over with immediately,' he vouched with wry amusement.

Jacy saw nothing amusing in the situation at all; her full lips tightened in a grim line. The past week had been sheer hell. On Tuesday Leo had dragged her to a Harley Street doctor, and her pregnancy was confirmed the same day. After that Leo had overridden her every objection like a steamroller flattening everything in its path. How he had convinced Liz and Tom of their hasty desire to marry she had no idea. But they had quite happily stood as witnesses at the ceremony. Leo—damn him!—had done his work well, she acknowledged. Even Liz, her best friend, had been totally convinced it was the love match of the decade.

The two girls had spent last night together and Jacy could have told Liz the true state of affairs, but her conscience wouldn't let her. She would not destroy Tom's career and she had no doubt that Leo would carry out his threat without a second thought. Suddenly it struck her as rather odd! Liz had made it easy for her. She had not been her usual inquisitive self at all last night, or this morning when the limousine had called at the house to collect them for the nine o'clock service. Liz had hurried her along with a few platitudes. Jacy had pinned a smile on her face and played her part to perfection. The wedding breakfast had been just that, except in the glamorous surroundings of the Dorchester Hotel.

A shaky sigh escaped her; now she was strapped into an aircraft seat next to Leo in the rear of an elegant lounge of a private jet, flying into a totally alien lifestyle with a man she despised. But did she? Deep in the secret corners of her mind a tiny voice reminded her that once her only wish in life had been to marry Leo.

'Are you worried at meeting my family again?' Leo reached for her hand, and she shrugged him off.

'Not in the least.'

'Then why the long sigh?'

'It's not every day one gets forced into marriage,' she said curtly.

'Keep your voice down.' She had not seen the cabin steward approaching. 'The world does not need to know of your childish grumbles.' Leo surveyed her with angry dark eyes. 'I don't find marriage any more agreeable than you do, but it is a necessity. Remember that...' The hard implacability of his tone brooked no argument, and she made none.

Leo ordered a whisky from the steward, adding, 'No alcohol for my wife. A cup of tea, perhaps?' He cast a sidelong, enquiring glance at Jacy.

'Nothing,' she snapped and, avoiding his eyes, she picked a magazine from the table in front of her and was soon deeply engrossed in an article on the European Community and the likelihood of the ECU eventually becoming the sole European currency. When she had finished she looked up and found Leo watching her, a strange expression in his eyes.

'You loved your work, didn't you?'

'I still do,' Jacy said bitterly, recalling the way he had calmly walked into her managing director's office last Wednesday afternoon and informed her boss she was leaving immediately.

They had argued all the way back to her mews cottage until finally Leo had snarled, 'You are carrying my child, albeit reluctantly. There is no way I am letting you out of my sight until the birth. I don't trust you.'

Knowing he actually believed she would try to get rid of the baby at the first available opportunity hurt her more than she was prepared to admit, and his closing comment, 'Think of Tom,' shut her up completely.

Dismissing her troubled memories, she glanced briefly at Leo and caught a glimpse of something oddly like compassion in his brown eyes, but it was angry resentment that made her answer his question spitefully. 'Hopefully in twelve months' time I will return to it, if not before.'

Long fingers caught her chin. 'Dismiss that idea from your mind; as my wife, you will stay by my side.' And she sensed it wasn't his side he had in mind. His face was much too close to her own, and with only a few inches between them she was vitally aware of his raw masculine appeal...

'Chauvinist,' she flung bitterly.

'I'm Greek; where my wife and child are concerned I freely admit to being chauvinistic. But you will not find me totally unreasonable. Mine is a large company; if at some later date you wish to work I will find something for you. Failing that, your boss has assured me he will quite happily give you some consultancy work, when you are able to do it.'

She was surprised and oddly flattered that Leo had actually discussed her resuming work with her boss, but she had no intention of telling him so.

'Am I supposed to thank you?' she gibed, her eyes icy-cold. 'Well, I'm not that generous. You've got a wife and hopefully in a few months a child. But that is all you're getting from me.'

'What are you trying to do, Jacy?' he raked in an undertone, his dark eyes narrowed angrily on her pale face. 'Turn our marriage into a war of the sexes before it has even had a chance? Well, it won't work.' And with the hand at her chin forcing her head back against the seat he leaned across her, and pressed his mouth to hers; his teeth bit down on her bottom lip and her mouth opened to give him entry.

She didn't want to respond; she caught her breath, trying to fight back the flood of feeling that threatened to engulf her, but Leo, with a throaty chuckle, merely increased the pressure, while his other hand slipped the jacket of her classic cream Calvin Klein suit open to caress her breast through the fine silk of the pale peach camisole.

'Stop it,' she whispered breathlessly.

Leo released her and leant back in his own seat. 'You're right,' he agreed with a triumphant smile. 'I can wait until tonight.' And, lowering his gaze to her breasts, the nipples outlined in stark relief against the fine fabric of her blouse, he added, 'But I'm not sure you can.'

Her face flamed and, dropping her head, she quickly fastened her jacket, then turned to look sightlessly out of the cabin window.

The Kozakis villa was enormous, set within what seemed to be miles of white walls. The limousine that had collected them from Corfu airport whisked them between massive wrought-iron gates, and up a long drive to the magnificent entrance portico. Dozens of cars were parked all along the drive. It looked as if half the island had turned out for the party.

'You look a little flustered. Don't worry; it will be fine,' Leo said softly, helping her out of the car. 'Trust me.'

'It's only the heat,' she defended swiftly, trying to disguise the mounting tension she felt. On the drive from the airport she had been vividly reminded of her first visit to Corfu. She had forgotten how beautiful the place was, the rocky hillsides covered with olive trees, and, to her surprise, the ground covered in a million different colourful spring flowers. Then there were the quaint villages, perched in the most unlikely places, and overall a hot, sweet fragrance peculiar to the island. She had not realised April would be so hot, and the light wool suit that had been perfectly acceptable for London was sticking to her back with perspiration.

Meekly allowing Leo to lead her up the large white steps to the front door, she ruefully acknowledged that sitting for the best part of an hour in the back seat of the car with Leo hadn't helped. She was disturbingly aware of his every move as, with complete disregard for her presence, he had busied himself on the journey with a pile of papers from his briefcase. Now, with his hand firmly curving her elbow, he ushered her inside.

The next few hours were sheer hell. The diamond-studded gold band Leo had placed on her finger earlier was marvelled over by what seemed to Jacy to be a thousand people. She gave up trying to remember the names after the first fifty or so. She had shed her jacket, but even the brief camisole with the shoe-string straps was beginning to cling to her.

Leo's father asked her to dance and teased her unmercifully. 'I knew you would marry my son. It was in your eyes the last time we danced, but you denied it.' And, patting her stomach, he laughed uproariously. 'But my Leo, he is all man; he always gets what he wants.'

'What was my father saying to you, Jacy?' Leo came up behind her and, placing his arms around her waist, he turned her around to face him.

She explained indignantly, and Leo laughed with the same masculine triumph as his father.

'It's not funny,' she fumed, the heat, the music and the crowd of laughing people making her head whirl.

'Poor Jacy, you look as bewildered as the first time I met you on the beach a couple of miles from here.' And she felt it, she realised solemnly. 'You have nothing to worry about; my family adore you.'

'I am surprised,' she drawled, nerves making her strike out at him sarcastically. 'I thought you Greeks only married virgins; I hardly fill the bill.'

His proud profile tautened. 'My father knows you were pure when we met. That is enough for him.'

'And does he know what you called me and how you dropped me like a ton of bricks?' she queried bitterly. Ten years ago this would have been the happiest day of her life. Now it was too late...

'I didn't deliberately set out to hurt you then. It was an unfortunate set of circumstances—a mistake, if you will. But now I have corrected the wrong I did you; what more could you want?'

The saddest part of all, Jacy realised, was that Leo was actually arrogant enough to believe what he said. 'Nothing, nothing at all,' she murmured, and he swept her into his arms and began to move to the haunting strains of the Greek love-song the band were playing.

With her slender hand held in his, the diamond band, its many facets sparkling brilliantly, caught her attention. To her surprise Leo had insisted on wearing a ring as well, a broad gold band. He moved her closer in his arms and she deliberately turned her head away, allowing her gaze to roam around the crowded room. Huge chandeliers hung from a high, ornately carved roof.

There were long, elegant windows from ceiling to floor,
the cerise silken drapes blowing in the breeze. The people
were all Greek, but not the stereotyped black-garbed
women of the travel brochure. This was a different world,
one of great wealth and designer dresses. The jewels of
the women alone were worth a king's ransom.

'You're slipping away from me, Jacy. I don't like it.'
Lost in her own thoughts, and oddly safe wrapped in
Leo's arms, she had let her mind wander, but, coming
back to the present with a shock, she was instantly aware
of the tension in his magnificent body. 'It is time we
left,' he said softly.

A great roar went up as Leo swept her up high in his
arms and, with an ease belying his huge frame, lightly
ran up a huge circular marble staircase. Jacy, her slender
arms wrapped around his neck, in self-preservation,
cried, 'What's going on?' All the guests were chasing
them.

Then they were inside a huge bedroom. Leo had
dropped her to her feet and speedily locked the door
behind him just as what sounded like a hundred fists
hammered on the door.

Catching her breath, she looked around in awe. In the
centre of the room was a huge carved and canopied bed,
a four-poster draped in pure white silk trimmed with gold
in the classic Greek design. The white walls were hung
with exquisite embroidered tapestries. The dressing-table
and wardrobes were of the finest yew, and obviously
antique. Intricate marquetry was inlaid on the finely
polished surfaces. The floor was an impressive marble
mosaic in blue and white, with huge rugs interrupting
the design around the bed. She caught sight of herself
in a long-mirrored door, and saw a stranger. Her golden
hair was brushed free and tumbling around her shoulders
in a mass of curls; the strap of her camisole was hanging
off one shoulder. She looked a mess, she thought

numbly, and she felt as nervous as any young virgin. How had it all happened? Where was her sophisticated, competent self?

'At last.' Two strong hands settled proprietorially on her slender shoulders, and spun her around.

She jumped and said the first thing that came into her head. 'Why the noise?' she asked breathlessly, and lifted her eyes to meet his. Her chest constricted in shock. He had stripped to a pair of black silk boxer shorts while she had been dumbly admiring the room, she realised, horrified... Instinctively she put up her hands to ward him off, but when her palms met the crisp hairs of his chest her fingers, with a will of their own, splayed with tactile delight in the seductive curls, the heat of his skin burning her fingertips.

'A tradition carried over from primitive days. Everyone at a wedding celebrates the moment of consummation. In ancient times they circled the bed.' His eyes gleamed with devilish humour. 'Now, thank God, voyeurism is out, and they stop at the door.'

She gasped, her eyes wide with horror at the picture his words portrayed. Then her gaze fastened on Leo, tall and bronzed, his muscular near-naked frame gleaming in the half-light, his head thrown back as he laughed out loud at her shocked expression. In that moment she fancied he looked like the devil himself, the white wings of hair at the side of his dark head resembling two horns. His eyes, black as jet, held hers with almost hypnotic fascination. His hands lifted to frame her face, raising it slightly, and she closed her eyes against the unmistakable passion burning in his.

'Open your eyes, Jacy,' he drawled throatily. 'There is nothing to be afraid of.'

'I'm tired.' And it was true, she realised, her long lashes fluttering briefly. She had been living on her nerves, in a state of permanent tension all day. No, not

just all day, but all week, and now she felt the last rem-
nants of her strength slipping away.

'I know, Jacy.' His voice softened huskily. 'I'll put
you to bed.'

Her eyes flickered open. What exactly did he mean?

Gently he reached for the straps of her top and slid
them off her arms; next he unclasped her bra, and then
his fingers unzipped her skirt and let it fall to the floor
before edging beneath the fine lace panties.

'Don't. I can't. No.'

'You would say no on our wedding night? Shame on
you, Jacy,' he mocked arrogantly, totally ignoring her
plea, his fingers easing her panties down over her thighs.

She knew exactly what he meant; he would put her to
bed all right, but with him. It was there in the dull flush
on his high cheekbones, the sensuous curving of his
mouth, and from somewhere she gathered her defeated
spirit, pushed hard against his chest, and stepped back.

'No, I said,' she cried. She would not let the arrogant
devil walk over her again! She would not give in to her
baser instincts, although her heartbeat raced and his
blatant masculine virility tempted her to do just that.
'I'm pregnant already; what the hell more do you want?'
She almost laughed at the expression of dumb
amazement that flashed across his handsome face, before
his eyes filled with icy anger.

'I want my wife in my bed, and using our child as an
excuse will not work. I know you...' And with ridiculous ease he caught her by the shoulders and in-
exorably drew her towards him. His raking, sexual,
explicit gaze appraised her near-naked form and left her
in no doubt of his intentions.

She began to struggle, but her bare breasts came in
contact with his broad chest, and his dark head descended to fasten with unerring accuracy over hers. She
opened her mouth to say no, but the denial died on her

lips as he began a ravaging exploration of her mouth that went on and on, until she felt the taste of her own blood on her tongue.

Then mercifully the kiss ended and she took great gulping gasps of air, but Leo, nowhere near as breathless as she was, swung her in his arms and deposited her on the bed. Quickly following her down, his splendidly muscled frame trapped her beneath him.

The dim glow of the bedside light outlined his harsh features. She gazed mutinously up at him, her golden eyes spitting fire.

'Why fight it, Jacy?' His heavy weight anchored her to the bed, and with one hand he caught her wrists and placed them above her head. His black eyes burned pitilessly down into hers. 'You want me, and I intend to show you just how much.' His head bent, but he did not kiss her, instead his lips touched her defiantly jutting chin and trailed down her throat to settle for a moment over the hollow that housed her madly beating pulse, then slipped lower to the softness of her breast.

His free hand skimmed down to cup the soft mound of her breast, rolling the tight nipple between finger and thumb at the same instant as his mouth covered its partner.

A spasm of agonising want shot through her trembling body; her back arched, offering her breasts to him, begging for his seductive caresses. Her golden eyes glazed and she gasped out loud, all thought of denial vanishing as his hand slid lower over her still flat stomach to the tangle of golden curls at her groin. One heavy muscled leg nudged between hers, spreading her thighs, as his fingers delved into the damp warmth of her female core.

He raised his head. 'You're my wife, and tonight we consummate our union,' he stated in a husky growl; his black eyes, simmering with heat, burnt into hers. 'In fact you will beg me to.'

Jacy wanted to refuse him. With her arms pinned above her head, his long length half over her, she felt like some primitive sacrifice from a classic Greek legend. Except that the hard, pulsating force of his own arousal pressed rigidly against her hip told her Leo was as help-lessly trapped, as much a slave to his passion as she was, and she was filled with a wild feminine satisfaction. Then his long fingers found the nub of her sexuality, and when he bent lower over her her lips parted provocatively. 'Make me,' she teased with an adult sensuality that she had never realised she possessed.

He reared up over her, setting her hands free to roam over the hard wall of his chest and lower to his narrow waist and the flat muscled stomach. He dragged her hands away and threw off his shorts. 'I never refuse a challenge,' he rasped, his hard-boned face taut with savage desire.

With one hand he spread her golden hair out over the white satin pillow. 'When I saw you at that party, I knew, I knew you would be mine again,' he groaned as his mouth covered hers in a long, drugging, passionate kiss, while all the time his other hand worked an erotic, sensuous magic on her tender flesh.

The blood raced through her veins like quicksilver, her breath strangled gasps between a moan or a whimper of ecstasy. The musky male scent of him filled her nostrils. She wanted him! Her small hand stroked down his stomach to his belly, desperate to touch him, but he caught her hand in his and placed it at her side.

'Not yet, Jacy! Tell me what you want.' His teeth bit on her tight, aching nipple, first one and then the other, and then in a soothing gesture he repeated the action with his tongue. 'What do you like?' he grated. 'Is it this?' And his mouth suckled her breast. 'Or perhaps this?' His fingers teased the hot, fluid centre of her.

Jacy cried out her need, her hand clawing around his waist and lower over his firm buttocks, urging him towards the ultimate act of possession. 'Yes, yes, please...' she begged, her body arched like a bow string, and with a muffled roar of masculine triumph Leo reared up and, sweeping her legs wide, lifted her up from the bed to accept his awesome male power. His mouth met hers in a frenzied all-consuming kiss as their two bodies locked into a rhythm uniquely their own.

Jacy woke up completely disorientated; her head felt fuzzy, and a great weight seemed to have settled over her waist. Her stomach churned and she wriggled, her bottom coming into contact with hard naked flesh. She heard a grunt and the events of last night came flooding back in sharp etched detail.

She stifled her own moan, not wanting to wake the sleeping Leo, and carefully moved towards the edge of the bed. Last night had been an education in the pleasures of the flesh; she would never forget it as long as she lived. How had she ever fooled herself into believing she could resist Leo? The question tormented her. He had taught her in the long hours of the night more about her own sexuality, her own wanton desires, until she had burnt in the fiery furnace of her own voracious appetite, avidly taking all he had to give and then greedily reciprocating in kind, until finally she had fallen asleep in his arms, satiated to the point of exhaustion.

She turned her head to look at him. His eyes were closed in sleep, his long, dark lashes curled over his hard cheekbones, his hair short, damp, ruffled curls on his broad brow. He looked younger and somehow defenceless. It was odd: they had been lovers years ago and again weeks ago, she was carrying his child, and yet this was the first time she had ever actually slept the night with him.

Her heart squeezed in her breast. 'My husband...' It was the first time she had said the word, and she lifted her hand to touch his face tenderly, then dropped it again. She swallowed hard as she thought about all the other women he must have spent the night with over the years. Simply because he had married her, it didn't make their relationship any different. A deep sadness welled up inside her, and with it the recognition she had tried to deny for years. She loved this man...always had...and probably always would... Fool that she was...

Her stomach churned, reminding her of her other foolishness, and, scrambling off the edge of the bed, she prepared to dash to the bathroom, but a large hand caught her wrist and forcefully dragged her back.

'No. Let go...' she cried, as she fell backwards on to the bed.

'No way. No woman cuts and runs on me,' Leo grunted angrily. 'Certainly not my wife.'

'You don't understand,' she tried to explain, her feet searching for and finding the floor, and with an almighty tug she was free and running for the bathroom, a hand over her mouth.

'Oh, God forgive me!' Leo leapt stark naked out of bed and caught her as she shot into the bathroom. With a strong arm protectively around her shoulder, his other around her stomach, he carefully held her while she was violently sick in the toilet bowl.

Jacy was utterly mortified, but too weak to object, as an oddly gentle Leo wrapped a large white fluffy towel around her naked body like a cocoon and sat her down on the bathroom stool. She watched fascinated as, totally unconscious of his own magnificent nudity, he put the plug in the large circular bath and turned on the taps. Then, rinsing a face cloth at the vanity basin, he came over and knelt in front of her. Taking her chin in his hand, he tenderly bathed her ashen face, talking all the time.

'I'm sorry, Jacy, truly I am. I forgot the baby; I never realised. I thought you were running... Hell, I don't know what I thought. I was just being my usual arrogant self and determined to keep you in my bed, until I said different.'

'It's all right,' she murmured, finally lifting her eyes to his face, and she was stunned to see the deep remorse in his dark brown eyes.

'Is it always like this?'

'Most mornings.'

'And I did this to you. You must hate me.' Straightening to his full height, he ran a tired hand through his rumpled hair. 'At this minute I don't much like myself,' he muttered.

For the next half-hour Jacy was treated to so much tender, loving care that she could hardly believe it. Leo insisted on helping her into the bath; he washed her hair with as much care as a mother would give a baby. He left her for a few minutes and she heard him giving staccato orders on the telephone. Then he was back and lifting her from the bath and, carefully wrapping her in another huge bath towel, he gently patted her dry, before carrying her back into the bedroom and tucking her tenderly back into the bed.

'Stay there and don't move.' He straightened, an impatient grimace twisting his hard mouth. 'Where the hell is the maid? I've already ordered the... tea and dry toast, isn't it...? I seem to remember the twins telling me.' He walked towards the door. 'I thought they exaggerated your sickness; now I know different. I'll see what the delay is.'

'Leo...' She said his name huskily.

'Yes?' He hesitated, a hand on the door.

Jacy started to smile, her honey-coloured eyes tracing over his magnificent body. 'Haven't you forgotten something?'

'What? Tell me.' His brown eyes, worried and flustered, searched her lovely face. 'Anything you want you can have.'

'Well, far be it from me to give you orders, Leo, but I think as your wife I would prefer you not to walk out of the door stark naked. I wouldn't want you frightening the staff.' And she burst out laughing as probably for the first time in his life the great Leo Kozakis blushed scarlet. Her laughter turned to a roar as she realised the blush wasn't confined to his face but suffused his whole body.

'Oh, hell.' He dashed across the room and into the bathroom, to reappear a second later in a short navy towelling robe. 'You could have mentioned it sooner, Jacy,' he opined, crossing to the bedside.

'What, and deprive myself of a sight for sore eyes? No way.' She chuckled and Leo's masculine laughter rang out to mingle with hers.

He reached over the bed, and pressed a light kiss to her forehead, still grinning. 'Now who's the voyeur? Behave yourself, woman, I'll be back.' And he sauntered out of the room.

Resting her head back against the pillow, Jacy felt better than she had in weeks. She loved Leo and she had finally admitted it to herself, but the question was what was she going to do about it? Using her analytical skills, she tackled the problem as she would a case.

On the positive side she listed: A, she was married to the man. B, he was a magnificent lover. C, he had shown her a tender, caring side to his nature. D, she knew he liked children—she had seen him with the twins—and so would love his own.

On the negative side: A, he did not love her. B, he was a womaniser and C, not above using blackmail to get his own way.

She sighed; the positive outweighed the negative, but only just. Jacy thought of Liz and Tom, and the surprise party. It was unbelievable that what had started as a stupid bet could make such a change in her life. She had gone out with Leo for a bet, and ended up married to him, which if she was honest was what she had probably subconsciously always wanted. So why not take another chance and continue her gamble? she asked herself. Leo might not love her, but he wanted her and she certainly wanted him. Time and propinquity, plus a child, and who knew? The solution was simple. This time she would gamble on passion and pray that she won Leo's love...

CHAPTER TEN

LEO returned almost immediately carrying a loaded tray bearing a china teapot, a delicate matching cup and saucer and plate, a full toast-rack and a variety of small pots of jam. Pride of place in the centre was a silver bud vase with one exquisite golden rose in it. She glanced up and caught the glint of humour in his dark eyes as he placed it carefully in front of her.

'Thank you.' She smiled, touched by his gesture, then cheekily added, 'If you used to serve the guests in the hotel wearing only a robe I bet all the women ordered breakfast in bed.'

Leo laughed. 'No, you lose the bet again. I reserve this service strictly for my wife.' Bending over her, he kissed the tip of her nose. 'But thank you for the compliment. I think it's the first nice thing you've said to me in weeks.'

He was right. 'I'll have to practise, then,' she murmured, her eyes lingering on his face, the dark early morning stubble giving him a piratical air.

'You don't need to practise, Jacy, you're perfect just as you are,' he responded throatily. 'Well, apart from your penchant for gambling,' he mocked, adding, 'Now eat your breakfast while I take a shower; you're much too tempting, and you've been sick.' Jacy chuckled when she heard him mutter worriedly under his breath, 'I must practise self-control,' as he headed for the bathroom.

It had been a marvellous honeymoon, Jacy thought tiredly as she stepped into the Jaguar at London airport.

They had stayed at Leo's uncle Nick's private island near Crete, where they had lived for one day at a time, swimming, laughing and making love.

She glanced lovingly at Leo sitting next to her, then yawned widely and closed her eyes. She had no idea how beautiful she looked. The sun had streaked her hair almost white in places, her creamy skin had developed a soft golden tan, and the man beside her glanced with unrestrained adoration at her sleeping form.

'Wake up, sleepyhead.'

She opened her eyes and stretched. They were parked outside the company apartment in Eaton Square. 'Back to the grind.' She smiled at Leo.

'Unfortunately that is true. I do have a lot of work to catch up on, and your monthly medical check is due.'

She had deliberately put it out of her mind in the euphoria of the past few weeks. Leo's reminder of the real reason for their marriage damped her spirit somewhat. But, walking into the apartment with Leo's hand curved around her elbow, and accepting the effusive congratulations of Mr and Mrs Belt, who looked after the place, before they left for the night, Jacy couldn't resist smugly congratulating herself. Her gamble appeared to be working. A more attentive husband didn't exist, she was sure, and, as for their sex life, it was just about perfect, day or night. She would feel Leo's eyes on her in a certain way and within minutes they were making love.

The only restraint she put on herself was that of silence; in the throes of passion sometimes she had to bite her tongue to prevent herself crying out her love. Leo, on the other hand, was a very verbal lover, but as he spoke in Greek she had no idea what he said. Once she had asked him to translate. He had joked, saying, 'You once told me not to speak dirty; you don't want to know.'

'Would you like a warm drink before we go to bed?' asked Leo now, his eyes narrowing faintly as they took in her sleepy features.

They had been watching the news on the television, and Jacy had found herself nodding off once or twice, lulled by the large beautifully cooked meal she had eaten courtesy of the Belts.

She lifted lazy eyes. 'No, I'm all right,' she refused, watching him, with feminine appreciation, walk to the drinks cabinet and pour himself a small whisky. He was lithe and compellingly masculine in dark trousers and a fine-knit shirt; suddenly she couldn't get to bed fast enough...

'You're sure?' He turned back to her, glass in hand, concern showing clearly in his dark, probing scrutiny. 'It's been a long day for you.'

His attentiveness warmed her heart, and various other places of her anatomy, she thought sexily. 'Yes,' she insisted huskily. 'I think I'll get an early night. I want to go home tomorrow. I forgot to ask my neighbour to water my plants. They're probably all dead by now.' She grimaced and, standing up, she threaded her hand through the wild tumble of her hair in an unconsciously provocative gesture.

'This is your home.' Leo slammed the glass he was holding down on the table, his dark eyes raking over her in glittering fury, his illusion of concern abruptly cast aside. 'And don't you forget it,' he commanded crushingly.

Suddenly the ease of the past three weeks vanished, and tension sizzled in the air.

Shock kept her immobile, that and a growing feeling of reciprocal anger at his high-handedness. She might be gambling on winning his love, but did that mean she had to turn herself into a doormat for the man? No way, she thought mutinously, and responded in kind. 'You don't give me orders!' She had not meant to shout, but she found some satisfaction in seeing the surprise in his autocratic features. 'And as for this being a home——' she waved a disparaging hand around the immaculate room '—it is a company apartment you admit yourself you rarely use. It makes much more sense to live in my house.' She hadn't actually thought about it until now, but suddenly the spirit that had made her a success in business had reasserted itself, the sensual daze she had been in for weeks was beginning to clear.

'This is where we will stay until I decide otherwise,' he declared icily, and stalked towards the door.

'But why? I have a perfectly good house, and you will be away a lot. I have neighbours   ' She trailed off, shaken by the cool detachment in his dark gaze as he turned, his hand on the door, and watched her stumble through her reasoning.

'You are my wife; you will do as I say,' he continued ruthlessly. 'Now I suggest you go to bed; you look tired. As for your house, I will make arrangements tomorrow for the sale of the property.'

Jacy bit her lip, anger giving way to hurt at his dismissive tone. Had the past few weeks meant nothing to him? She had fondly imagined they were growing closer, but now she was no longer so sure. 'That is unnecessary, Leo.' Crossing to him, she laid her hand on his arm. 'Surely you can see the sense of my proposal? It will be much better for me and my child,' she pressed.

'*Our* child. And I decide what is necessary. I don't wish to hear any more about it.' The dark-lashed black eyes clashed with hers, and his hand covered hers on his arm. 'Go to bed; I have work to do in the study. I will join you later.'

She said nothing. She was infuriated by his arrogant assumption that she would do exactly as he said, and afraid as the warmth of his hand on hers sent the all too familiar shivers of pleasure down her spine.

He carelessly brushed his other hand through her long hair, adding, 'I won't be long,' and her brief defiance vanished as her pulse raced hectically, anticipation curling in her stomach. He only had to touch her and she melted.

'Leo, about the house——' she began, lifting her free hand and running her fingers teasingly down his throat to his chest.

'Enough, woman.' His icy control broke, and he kissed her with hard hunger before thrusting her away. 'Don't try it,' he snarled.

'Try what?' she muttered shakily, still reeling from the unexpected force of his kiss.

'I will not be manipulated by sex, not even by you.' Swinging on his heel, he left, the door rocking on its hinges behind him.

Later, lying in the unfamiliar bed in a room decorated efficiently in shades of brown and blue, waiting for Leo to join her, Jacy silently seethed. She loved him, and yet he dared to accuse her of using sex to manipulate him. If anything, the reverse was true. It was Leo who managed to get his own way every time simply because she could not say no to him.

How long she could continue with the gamble that her love would be returned she did not know, but she had a sinking feeling that this was one bet she was not going to win. She knew herself well enough to realise she was not cut out to play the little *hausfrau*. Eventually Leo, with his abrupt mood swings, and his arrogant assumption that she would obey his every whim, would try her temper too far.

A humourless smile curved her lips. She had always known Leo was ruthless, but because of her love for him and their unborn child she bit her tongue and held her

temper. But her patience wasn't finite—anything but...
Eventually she fell into an uneasy sleep alone. But in
the morning she awoke to find Leo standing by the side
of the bed, staring down at her, a cup of tea in his hand.

He was wearing an immaculate charcoal-grey business
suit. His handsome face, tanned even deeper by their
holiday in the sun, was somehow remote. But to Jacy
he looked every inch the perfect male animal, and her
heart expanded with love. Still drowsy, she reached a
hand out sleepily. 'Come to bed.'

'Sorry—work.' Lowering his dark head, he kissed her
lightly on the cheek, adding perfectly calmly, as though
he were addressing a board meeting, 'Don't go out
without telling me where you're going. Here is my
number. Ring if you want anything.' And, pressing a
piece of paper in her hand, he left.

It was all very well for Leo; he had his work to keep
him occupied, Jacy thought a few days later, but for her
it was a vast adjustment from being a busy career girl
to lying around in an apartment all day. Leo had taken
her out twice, once to the doctor for her medical check,
and once on a very expensive shopping spree in
Kensington, culminating in lunch in a small Italian bistro
next to the Kozakis office block. He had bundled her
into a taxi and sent her home, but he rarely managed to
get home himself before eight, and the apartment was
beginning to feel like a prison.

On impulse she rang Liz and after an exchange of
greetings she made a date to meet her the same day for
afternoon tea at Harrods. Feeling much better, she
bathed, washed her hair, and really went to town on her
make-up. Even so, she was ready before noon.

She wandered around the empty apartment and,
catching sight of herself in the large mirror in the hall,
thought, Not bad, Jacy! Her skin was still tanned a nice
golden brown from her honeymoon and her sun-streaked

hair was brushed back from her face and tied with a silk scarf to fall in a curling ponytail down her back. She was wearing one of the new outfits Leo had chosen and paid for, a pale blue and yellow patterned silk blouson jacket with a plain blue sleeveless scooped-neck blouse and matching patterned culottes. It was a lovely summer May day and she wore no stockings, just low-heeled strappy blue sandals. Her only jewellery was the pendant Leo had given her; she had retrieved it from the bathroom floor weeks ago and remembering the angry scene that had followed at the time, she had an urge to see Leo. Her insecurities were showing, she knew, but what the hell! He was her husband. She knew where his office was. Why not?

The decision made, she walked jauntily out of the apartment, and hailed a cab. She would surprise him; they could eat at the little bistro again and then she would go on and meet Liz for tea. After all, she was feeding two; she could afford to make a pig of herself for once.

An hour later, as she turned the key in the lock of her own house, food was the furthest thing from her mind. Pale and shaking, she staggered to the bedroom and fell down on the bed, the tears rolling helplessly down her cheeks.

She cried and cried, great racking sobs that shook her whole body. She bent her knees up to her chest and wrapped her arms around them. Curved into a near foetal position, she wept until there were no more tears. Her throat dry and parched, her head aching, she finally turned over on to her back and lay staring sightlessly at the ceiling.

Jacy couldn't believe the pain; it seared her flesh like a million lash strokes. In her mind's eye she saw once again the entrance to Kozakis House, the impressive office block in the centre of the city. The glass doors parted automatically and out on to the pavement stepped

a couple. The man, tall and dark, his handsome face
wreathed in smiles, turned his head to the blonde woman,
and, curving an arm around her shoulders, kissed her
cheek. Leo and Thelma...

Like a spectre at a feast Jacy saw herself fall back
against the wall of the building and watch them stroll
along the street and turn into the entrance of a familiar
restaurant.

Betrayal... Deception... Emotive words, but who was
at fault? she asked herself brutally. Her husband of a
few weeks had betrayed her with another woman, but
she could not accuse him of deception. He had made
no promise to love her. He had married her for the child
she was carrying. He had quite openly blackmailed her
into the marriage; he had not tried to deceive her with
soft words or avowals of undying love.

No, she had done that herself. Deliberately she had
deceived herself, by imagining that their marriage was
anything other than a convenient deal between two
people responsible for a child. She had betrayed herself,
the strong, mature Jacy with a clear knowledge of her
own self-worth, which she had deliberately suppressed
in a futile gamble to win the love of a man who wasn't
worthy of her love.

Sitting up, she swung her feet to the floor and,
sweeping her tangled mass of hair from her face, she
cupped her head in her hands. How could she have been
such a complete and utter idiot? Leo was a highly sexed
virile man. Last night he had not touched her, now she
knew why: he had a date for today... He could afford
to go without for a few hours. It was that basic, that
simple...

Getting to her feet, she looked around the familiar
room. A photograph of her father in a brass frame had
pride of place on the bedside table. She stared at it for
a moment, remembering the first time Leo had betrayed

her, and how she had found comfort and strength from
her father. He might have been wrong about the
palimony case, but he had been right in his reading of
Leo's character; of that she had no doubt. When she
was eighteen he had warned her. God! The cry was from
her very soul; how she wished she had heeded the
warning.

But it wasn't too late, she vowed silently. Her parents
had brought her up to be strong and independent. Was
she going to disgrace their memory by wallowing in despair and self-pity? No way! She ran a hand over the
soft swell of her stomach; this was her baby, their grand-
child. For the baby's sake she would survive the heart-
break, and the first thing she needed to do was eat. The
empty feeling in her stomach was not just despair but a
genuine need for sustenance.

She made her way downstairs and stopped in her
living-room, and looked with dismay at the row of large
packing-cases stacked against one wall. Another sign of
her spineless behaviour where Leo was concerned. Rather
than argue with him again, she had meekly handed him
a key for the house and allowed him to arrange the sale.

With his usual ruthless efficiency he had obviously
already contacted the removal firm to have her personal
things packed. A slow-burning anger built up inside her
and erupted in fury.

'The bastard. The low-down, arrogant, over-sexed
bastard,' she swore out loud. 'Well, this time the swine
is not going to have his way.'

Her violent outburst acted like a catharsis. She could
see things clearly at last. She had come to her senses just
in time. She still had her home, and here she was staying.
Even if she had to fight Leo Kozakis in every court
in the land, she would keep her child and
her independence . . .

The decision made, she took a few deep, calming breaths, and an icy calm pervaded her being. Blank-faced, she crossed to the mantelpiece and picked up one of a group of tiny little figures, a dragon's head, the first *netsuke* she had acquired, as a present from her father. She turned the smooth ivory figure over in the palm of her hand. Who would believe the desire for such a tiny object could bring so much pain? Perhaps it was fitting, she thought with irony, replacing the dragon on the mantel. The ivory trade was a disgusting business; maybe it was only right the recipients of the dirty business should feel some pain. And she knew in that moment that she would never buy another *netsuke*...

The sound of fists thundering on her front door stilled her hand for a second before she continued methodically raising the fork to her mouth and eating the dish of baked beans set in front of her on the kitchen table. It was all she had been able to find in the near-empty cupboards. But the sound of Leo's angry voice shouting to her to open the door did get through to her.

'Jacy, are you there? Are you all right?'

She stopped and replaced the fork in the dish, her hand shaking. He actually sounded as if he cared. What a liar! 'Get lost,' she screamed back, not actually expecting him to hear her, but it made her feel better...

The pounding on the door intensified. 'Open this door, Jacy. What the hell are you playing at? Liz was worried sick when you didn't turn up.'

Tea! She'd forgotten all about it. She might have guessed Liz would call Leo, and of course he had to play the caring husband and come looking for her. What a joke! She stood up and, rinsing her plate under the tap in the sink, walked slowly through to the hall. She was going to bed, and he could hammer till doomsday for all she cared.

'Jacy, if you don't open this door I will break it down.'

Jacy hesitated, her foot on the first stair, and thought about it for a second. He would do it, she didn't doubt. Turning around, she straightened her shoulders, and, head high, she marched to the door. If it was a confrontation Leo wanted, that was what he would get. Hadn't she spent the last hour convincing herself she was worth more than what Leo was offering, and determining to do something about it? Well, now was the time to start. No longer was she a slave to his sexual expertise; she could learn to live without him, and the sooner she began, the better.

She flung open the door and Leo was captured with a fist up above his head. 'Lost your key, Leo?' She had given him it only yesterday. 'But then I shouldn't be surprised; after all, you must have an awful lot to juggle with,' she opined with thinly veiled contempt. He must have the keys to more women's apartments than a locksmith!

'What the hell are you talking about?' he said in a hard voice, lowering his hand to his side. 'And why did you stand Liz up? She waited two hours for you. She was worried about you and called me.'

She stared at him. He had changed from the suit he had left the apartment in that morning into a soft denim shirt and jeans. For a second she wondered if it had been for Thelma's benefit, and frowned, before responding. 'Sorry you've been troubled, but, as you can see, I am perfectly OK.' The words were clipped and she had to stifle the desire, even now when he had hurt her beyond belief, to reach out and touch him. The first three buttons of his shirt were open, his hair was rumpled, and he needed a shave, but even so he exuded a raw animal magnetism that it took all her strength to ignore.

His rapier-like glance raked her from head to toe as though he had never seen her before. 'And of course it never once occurred to you to inform me where you were going,' he drawled derisively.

'No, why should I? You're not my keeper.' With a defiant toss of her head she turned on her heel, and would have slammed the door in his face, but she was too slow...

Leo grabbed her around the waist, swung her high in the air, and carried her across the hall and into the living-room. She struggled furiously, her arms flailing wildly, but with her back to his chest she had nothing to strike out at. He spun her around to face him, and for an instant desire flared between them, but brutally she crushed it.

'Let me go,' she said curtly.

Leo's mouth curled. 'Over my dead body.' His grip tightened on her upper arms, his dark eyes narrowed assessingly on her pale face. 'Now what happened? You are not OK. You've been crying; your eyes are red. What the hell are you playing at, Jacy? I demand an explanation.'

He demanded! And of course what the great Leo Kozakis wanted he got, she thought bitterly. Well, not this time. And, schooling her features into what she hoped was cool disdain, she responded by acting for all she was worth.

'It is quite simple, Leo. I have decided to live here in my own house. I'm sorry I forgot about Liz, but I will call her and apologise. As for the red-rimmed eyes, I was looking at a photograph of my father; it's the anniversary of his death this week,' she improvised quickly. His touch was getting to her again, and, clenching her hands at her sides, she evaded his eyes as she continued, 'Maudlin, I know, but...' She tried to shrug, and swallowed hard. The silence seemed to stretch interminably between them.

Finally Jacy had to look up at him, and choked back a gasp at the expression on his hard face. She had expected him to lose his temper, rant and rave. Instead his dark brown eyes were curiously empty, but in the emptiness she glimpsed an edge of... was it torment?

He was staring at her and when he finally broke the tense silence even his voice sounded different, defeated. 'All right, Jacy, we will live here for now.' Letting go of her arms, he turned and lowered his long frame on to the sofa.

Her mouth fell open in shock. She shook her head to try and clear it, her long hair flying around her face. What did he mean, *we* will live here?

'Do you think I could have a coffee? I left the apartment in rather a hurry.' He shot her a wry glance. 'Obviously I need not have worried about you; you appear to have everything under control.'

Jacy took a step forward to stand in front of him. 'No. No...' she repeated desperately. This wasn't supposed to happen. Leo had to go.

'No coffee.' One black brow arched sardonically. 'And I have to give up a luxury apartment for this? Tut tut.' He shook his head mockingly, and Jacy saw red.

He wasn't defeated. He wasn't tormented. He was his usual bloody-minded arrogant self, and laughing at her to boot. In a split second something seemed to snap in Jacy. Tears of rage half blinded her, and she jumped on him like a wildcat. Her hands curled into fists, she hit out at his cold face. She was bitterly angry, thwarted by his bland acceptance of her story, and filled with burning jealousy and resentment.

Leo's hands gripped her wrists, and with insulting ease he swung her on to the sofa and pinned her beneath him.

'Get off me,' she screamed. 'You bastard.' She bucked wildly beneath him. 'You lecherous old goat, pig...' She screamed at him every vile name she could think of and then some, before he bent his black head and shut her mouth with his. His mouth burnt hers, his hard body pressing her into the sofa as the kiss grew deeper, more urgent, until with a despairing moan she felt herself succumb, liquid fire flowing through her veins with an urgency that was terrifying. Her head spun and she reached up to him, her hands sliding around his neck.

Leo ended the kiss, lifting his head. His gaze burnt on her swollen mouth for a second, then he slowly raised his black eyes to hers. 'Name-calling won't help you,' he said thickly, an edge of steel in his tone. 'I want the truth. You were running, and I want to know why.'

He wanted the truth, the one thing she could not give him; she had too much pride. She could not speak.

Leo moved to one side, his big body urging hers against the back of the sofa. He flung a heavy thigh over her slender legs, keeping her prisoner, but relieving her of his weight. 'Not the mute treatment again, Jacy; it won't work. I know I'm no expert with women—you only have to look at my track record to realise that—but——'

'You're joking, of course,' she prompted snidely, but Leo did not take her up on her sarcasm.

'No. But I honestly thought since you and I married I had finally got it right. You accepted me as your husband although I know I was less than honourable in blackmailing you into marriage. I thought we were making a go of it. But tonight when I returned to the apartment and discovered you'd gone I couldn't believe it. I almost went crazy when Liz rang. I have just spent the worst few hours of my life, imagining you hurt or worse. I rang all the hospitals before I thought of here.'

She wanted to believe his concern was genuine, but she didn't dare. She stared at him in silence, and felt the rapid beat of her heart quicken. Leo slid his hand to her neck, and he watched her intently as he felt the tell-tale beat of her pulse in her throat.

'You want me.' His thigh moved restlessly over her long legs, his arm around the end of the sofa slipped beneath her head, and he urged her face up to his. His lips brushed hers. 'Sex has never been a problem with us, so tell me what's wrong, Jacy.' For an agonising moment she was tempted to pour her heart out, but fear of further humiliation stopped her.

'Haven't you realised yet? I would do anything in the world for you,' he murmured against her lips. 'But I need to know what you want, what you need.' And all the time his hand strayed lower to stroke lightly over her breast.

His hands, his voice, the pressure of his hard body were all seducing her. She tilted her head back and her eyes met his, and she was mesmerised by what she saw there. His ruggedly attractive face was taut with some unbearable pain and his black eyes glittered as if with fever.

'I love you, Jacy,' he said in a raw voice. 'You're the best thing that's ever happened to me, and I don't want to lose you.'

Jacy was too choked to speak. She began to tremble violently, and his arm tightened about her, drawing her more firmly against his muscular body.

'For God's sake, Jacy, say something. I'm baring my soul here, and you——'

'Is it true?' she said shakily. 'You love me?'

Leo stared at her fixedly, his body rigid. 'God, you know I do. I've told you a hundred times every time we've made love. I married you. How can you doubt it?'

She wanted to believe him, more than life, but... 'I thought it was only because of the baby.'

He stared at her for a moment in shocked disbelief, and then he laughed, a harsh, mocking sound devoid of all amusement. 'Your opinion of me is so low, you might as well know it all. I got you pregnant deliberately; at least I hoped I had.'

'What?' She gasped. Though, thinking back, it was strange that Leo, who had made such a point of being protected the first time they had ever loved, should ignore the same precautions when they were both much older and wiser... 'You did it deliberately?' The enormity of his admission stunned her.

'Yes. I know—despicable of me. But from the first time I saw you again at Liz's I determined to have you for myself. I thought I had succeeded that night in my apartment when we cleared up the mistakes about the past and would have made love but for the telephone call. When I was in America I lived every day for the sound of your voice, and when I returned to London I couldn't wait to see you, and I thought you felt the same.'

'I did,' she said without thinking.

'But you went out with me for a bet,' Leo reminded her, drawing away to look intently down at her. 'I knew all along, but it didn't stop me wanting you. When I made love to you that night it was stupid male ego that made me throw the knowledge of the bet in your face. I knew I had to return to Corfu and I thought it would do you no harm to lose the bet, and I'd be back in a week and we'd take up where we left off. Unfortunately I got held up in Corfu. But I can't regret that night; because of it you married me.'

'And a little blackmail,' Jacy teased. Suddenly her heart felt lighter and she snuggled into his hard warmth. She felt his lips against her hair, and then they dropped lower to brush against her ear, and a shiver of pleasure raced down her spine.

'Blackmail aside——' he tilted her chin with one finger and gave her a crooked smile '—I thought I had won. In and out of bed, you're everything and more than I ever dreamed of.' His dark eyes, the pupils dilating to almost black, seared hers as he reached up and ran his fingers through the silken mass of her hair, sweeping it back from her brow. 'I'm not asking for your love, Jacy—I know I don't deserve it—but I want you to stay with me.' He crushed her against him and groaned into her fragrant hair. 'I went through the torment of the damned tonight when you disappeared and I don't think I could stand it a second time.'

Jacy tried to speak, but couldn't for the emotion that blocked her throat. She swallowed hard, and Leo eased her back against the cushion. She searched his face for the truth. The rigidity of his features was betrayed by a muscle jerking wildly under the dark skin. Her golden eyes clashed with his and for a second she saw his heart in his eyes, the mask of cool arrogance stripped away to reveal the vulnerable man beneath.

She believed him. 'Leo...' she breathed, but he did not seem to hear, too intent on his confession.

'So if living here means so much to you, we will. Because there is no way on God's earth I will let you go.' His dark head lowered, his hand once more dipping to cup her breast. She felt the curling of desire and closed her eyes, lifting eager lips to his. He loved her. He would never let her go. They would live here... Then the reason she was here in the first place hit her, and with an almighty shove she dislodged him from the sofa.

'My God,' she exclaimed, her voice cracking with fury, unconcerned that Leo was lying flat on his back on the floor. 'I almost fell for it... And to think you accused me of sexual manipulation. Love? You don't know the meaning of the word. I saw you today with your girl-friend Thelma. What do you take me for—a complete

idiot?' She was shouting, but didn't care. She never saw
the look of incredulity on Leo's face as she swung her
feet to the floor and sat up.

'Thelma? That's what this is all about.' And, tossing
his head back, he roared with laughter.

Flushed, dishevelled and furious, Jacy jumped to her
feet. His laughter was the last straw, and she aimed a
hefty kick at his most vulnerable part, but before she
could connect Leo had caught her ankle and brought
her tumbling down on top of him. His arms closed
around her in a vice-like grip and her face was buried
on his chest. The curling body hair through the open
neck of his shirt tickled her nose and she tried to raise
her head. She got one arm free and planted it on his
shoulder to push herself up, but his long legs twined with
hers and she was caught between his thighs.

'You fight dirty, Jacy.' His triumphant smile beamed
up at her. 'We are a lot alike, you and I.' And, tangling
his hand in her long hair, he forced her head down to
meet his mouth.

Jacy tried to fight it, but it was no use. Sprawled on
top of him, their bodies provocatively entwined, she felt
her last shred of anger vanish in the wonder of his kiss...

'You were jealous, you little she-cat,' he murmured
against her lips. 'You've no idea how great that makes
me feel.' He pulled her head back and his darkening eyes
searched her flushed face. Recognising her uncertainty,
he continued, 'You had no need, my love. I don't know
what you saw.'

'You and Thelma walking out of the office; you kissed
her.' She wanted there to be an explanation, but she had
been hurt too much by this man already.

'Jacy, I have never, ever even thought of being un-
faithful to you, not from the first moment I saw you
again at Liz's.'

'But I saw you...' It was a cry from the heart.

'You saw me with an arm around the shoulder of a woman who I had just congratulated on doing some excellent work for me, hence the kiss on the cheek—and that was all it was.'

'What work?' she asked suspiciously.

Leo chuckled, his dark eyes lit with laughter. 'I suppose I will have to tell you, but it blows my surprise. You know when we collected the boys from Sunday school that day...well, did you notice the old vicarage with the scaffolding around it?' he asked, but, without waiting for her reply, continued, 'Anyway, it's a large stone-built house set in a small wood a hundred yards down the road.'

'Yes, but what's——?'

'Shut up and listen.' But the quirk of his lips belied his serious tone. 'When I was in America I arranged with Tom to buy the vicarage, and Tom put me in touch with a local builder and hired Thelma, as the best interior designer, to get a woman's opinion on what you would like.'

She stared at Leo dumbly, unable to speak. His brown eyes watched her with a compelling intensity, as if willing her to believe him. 'You bought a house for us, near Tom and Liz? When you were in America, before you even knew...' She spoke her thoughts out loud. 'You were that sure...'

'I've always known from the day I met an eighteen-year-old on the beach at Paleokastritsa, only it has taken me until just recently to finally admit it. I thought you knew how I felt on our first date, when I introduced you to my family.'

'Your father asked me if I was going to marry you...' she remembered.

'I know; I had already told him of my intentions. I had lost you once and I swore I would not let you slip through my fingers again. I tried to tell you how I felt when I called you from America. I hinted I wanted a family.' His strong fingers picked up the pendant that hung at her neck. 'I bought you this as a symbol. You had my heart. But I am ashamed to say I still did not quite trust you; this house, the bet, rankled with me. I have never been so relieved as when you told me your father left you the house, but the damage between us was already done when you let slip that piece of information,' he chided gently, and she had the grace to blush.

'I should have put you right straight away, but you were so contemptuous that I got angry...'

'Anyway, when we made love here in this house I still hadn't the courage to openly declare my love; instead I hid my feelings behind taunting you with the bet and sarcastic comments about your lifestyle, but I seem to recall I let slip that, with every woman I'd tried to bed in the last ten years, the face on the pillow had always been yours. Why did you think I always dated blondes? Before I met you my preference was for brunettes.'

'Really? I'm flattered, I think...'

His dark eyes fused with hers. 'If I had thought for one second I would be away from you another three weeks I would never have behaved with such conceited arrogance. Please, Jacy, say you forgive me.'

'There is nothing to forgive.' She sighed and licked the skin showing through the open neck of his shirt.

'You're very generous,' he rasped huskily, his arms tightening around her. He buried his head in her sweet-smelling hair.

Jacy realised she believed him, and, if he was telling the truth about loving her, then surely it followed that he was also telling the truth about Thelma. Suddenly her heart felt lighter. Her golden eyes shone with love as she lifted her head and smiled down at him. 'You bought a house for us.' Only one thing bothered her. 'Then why were you so adamant we had to stay in the apartment? If we are going to have a home in the country, surely we could just as easily have stayed here?'

Leo sighed and stroked his hands tenderly up her back, but his brown eyes avoided her questing gaze, fixing on some point on the ceiling, almost as if he was afraid to look at her. 'Jealousy. You've lived here alone a long time, and the thought of sharing the same bed you've shared with other men...'

Jacy began to chuckle. Her head fell down on his chest and she curved her slender arms around him, hugging him to her. 'You fool,' she admonished, a wide grin enhancing her beautiful face. 'I told you once—no man has ever slept in my bed but you.'

'You called me a chauvinist and I am. I know it's old-fashioned... What did you say...?' Suddenly her words had registered and in a second he had rolled her over on to her back, his large body poised darkly above her, but the glitter in his deep brown eyes was not in the least threatening. 'You never...'

'No, never! I loved you at eighteen and I never stopped.' The look of wonder and love on his bronzed face made her heart sing, and she knew he deserved it all. 'I didn't go out with you just for the bet; in fact when I saw you were the first man in the room I told Liz the bet was off. But you got under my skin with your arrogant assumption that because I was no longer supposedly a reporter I was all right to date.'

'Was I that bad?'

'Yes, but I knew when you went to America I wanted you back. I tried to tell myself it wasn't love, simply that I had spent too long celibate, and it was time I joined the adult world and plunged into a relationship. Only it didn't work. After the night we made love I was furious and felt used and vowed to forget about you all over again.'

'I know; I could have killed you when you turned down my date for the opera and turned up with that red-haired Adonis. Thank God I found out about him before I destroyed him.'

Jacy's eyes widened in surprise. The arrogant Leo was back with a vengeance. 'Destroyed him?'

'I thought about it until the investigator told me he was a homosexual, so I let it go.'

'You are ruthless, Leo,' she said uncertainly. She didn't like the idea that he had investigated Simon, but somehow it did not surprise her.

'Only to protect the people I love, Jacy.' And, swooping down, he pressed a soft kiss to her parted lips.

For a long time the only sound in the darkening room was that of clothes being hastily discarded, and then Leo's deep, melodious voice, sounding like the rustle of satin sheets, huskily declaring all the erotic delights in store, and to Jacy the floor became the most luxurious bed as she gave herself up to her husband's loving...

Later, lying enfolded in his arms, she smiled mischievously up at him. 'Well, you weren't a bad bet after all, Leo. But tell me, what would you have done if I wasn't pregnant, and didn't have to marry you?'

He didn't return her smile; instead he sat up and turned his body to stare down at where she lay naked on the carpet, a flash of anguish in his deep brown eyes. 'Does it bother you that I forced you into this marriage and the baby?'

'No, oh, no. And you were wrong, you know, Leo; I never even considered getting rid of the baby.'

'I think I always knew that, but it was another way to keep you at my side.'

Jacy knelt up beside him and wrapped her slender arms around his strong neck, pressing tiny kisses to his cheek, and chin, anywhere she could reach. 'I love you, and I finally admitted it to myself on our wedding night. In fact I made another bet.'

'You what?' His roar shook the house. 'Who with this time? Not Liz, because I confessed everything to her days before our wedding.'

So that was why Liz was so reticent the night before the marriage, Jacy realised, but all such thoughts were knocked out of her head by Leo hauling her to her feet.

He clasped her hands to his naked chest. 'Gambling is a mug's game, Jacy,' he said urgently. 'What was it this time?' he demanded, and she could feel the heavy thud of his heart beneath her clasped hands. 'I'll find out and cancel it; your betting has caused us both enough heartache already.'

She looked up at him with a secret smile playing around her full lips, and sighed dramatically. 'Cancel it, you say... Well, if you insist.'

'I'm your husband; I do insist.'

'It seems a shame,' she murmured, her eyes lingering over his naked body in deliberate sensual invitation. She freed her hand and stroked down his chest and lower to his flat muscled stomach. She heard his stifled moan of pleasure, and her cheeks dimpled in a wicked smile at the sight of his obvious masculine response. 'I do enjoy gambling.' She tapped him lightly and stepped back.

'Jacy...' He gasped and reached for her.

She lifted molten golden eyes to his, and murmured, 'On the first day of our marriage I gambled on passion making our marriage work, but as an obedient wife I bow to your superior judgement,' and burst out laughing.

'You witch.' Leo laughed, shaking his head in disbelief, and, grabbing her around the waist, he kissed her until she clung to him. Then he lifted his dark head, gently brushed back a lock of unruly hair from her brow, and stared at her, his black eyes leaping with devilment and banked-down desire.

'Well, I am an extremely wealthy man, Jacy, darling,' he drawled throatily as his hand slid to her hips and pulled her in tight against his thighs. 'Perhaps I was a bit hasty. You can gamble every day of your life, as long as it's only with me.'

HARLEQUIN PRESENTS®

It's getting hotter!
Look out for our sizzling selection of stories...

They're

Coming next month:
Dark Fire by Robyn Donald
Harlequin Presents #1735

From the moment they met, Flint Jansen had shattered
Aura's world. She found him overwhelmingly attractive,
powerfully charismatic...but she was already engaged to his
friend Paul! She now faced a battle with her conscience,
and with Flint: he demanded that she cancel the wedding
and succumb to his dark seduction. In the heat of a tropical
night, would Aura's resistance melt?

Available in April wherever Harlequin books are sold.

THTH-3R

MILLION DOLLAR SWEEPSTAKES (III)

No purchase necessary. To enter, follow the directions published. Method of entry may vary. For eligibility, entries must be received no later than March 31, 1996. No liability is assumed for printing errors, lost, late or misdirected entries. Odds of winning are determined by the number of eligible entries distributed and received. Prizewinners will be determined no later than June 30, 1996.

Sweepstakes open to residents of the U.S. (except Puerto Rico), Canada, Europe and Taiwan who are 18 years of age or older. All applicable laws and regulations apply. Sweepstakes offer void wherever prohibited by law. Values of all prizes are in U.S. currency. This sweepstakes is presented by Torstar Corp., its subsidiaries and affiliates, in conjunction with book, merchandise and/or product offerings. For a copy of the Official Rules send a self-addressed, stamped envelope (WA residents need not affix return postage) to: MILLION DOLLAR SWEEPSTAKES (III) Rules, P.O. Box 4573, Blair, NE 68009, USA.

EXTRA BONUS PRIZE DRAWING

No purchase necessary. The Extra Bonus Prize will be awarded in a random drawing to be conducted no later than 5/30/96 from among all entries received. To qualify, entries must be received by 3/31/96 and comply with published directions. Drawing open to residents of the U.S. (except Puerto Rico), Canada, Europe and Taiwan who are 18 years of age or older. All applicable laws and regulations apply, offer void wherever prohibited by law. Odds of winning are dependent upon number of eligible entries received. Prize is valued in U.S. currency. The offer is presented by Torstar Corp., its subsidiaries and affiliates in conjunction with book, merchandise and/or product offering. For a copy of the Official Rules governing this sweepstakes, send a self-addressed, stamped envelope (WA residents need not affix return postage) to: Extra Bonus Prize Drawing Rules, P.O. Box 4590, Blair, NE 68009, USA.

SWP-H395

HARLEQUIN®

PRESENTS *Plus*

"Virgin or wanton?" Oliver Lee is suspicious of everything and everyone.... When he meets Fliss, he thinks her innocence is an act. Fliss *may* be innocent, but the passion Oliver inspires in her is just like raw silk—beautiful, unique and desirable. But like raw silk it is fragile....Only love will help it survive.

Ben Claremont seemed to be the only man in the world who didn't lust after Honey's body...but he asked her to marry him anyway! Honey wasn't in love with him—so separate rooms would suit her just fine! But what on earth had she gotten herself into? Were their wedding vows based on a lie?

Presents Plus—the Power of Passion!

Coming next month:

Raw Silk by Anne Mather
Harlequin Presents Plus #1731

and

Separate Rooms by Diana Hamilton
Harlequin Presents Plus #1732

Harlequin Presents Plus
The best has just gotten better!

Available in April wherever Harlequin books are sold.

HARLEQUIN®

Don't miss these Harlequin favorites by some of our most distinguished authors!
And now, you can receive a discount by ordering two or more titles!

HT#25577	WILD LIKE THE WIND by Janice Kaiser	$2.99	☐
HT#25589	THE RETURN OF CAINE O'HALLORAN by JoAnn Ross	$2.99	☐
HP#11626	THE SEDUCTION STAKES by Lindsay Armstrong	$2.99	☐
HP#11647	GIVE A MAN A BAD NAME by Roberta Leigh	$2.99	☐
HR#03293	THE MAN WHO CAME FOR CHRISTMAS by Bethany Campbell	$2.89	☐
HR#03308	RELATIVE VALUES by Jessica Steele	$2.89	☐
SR#70589	CANDY KISSES by Muriel Jensen	$3.50	☐
SR#70598	WEDDING INVITATION by Marisa Carroll	$3.50 U.S. $3.99 CAN.	☐
HI#22230	CACHE POOR by Margaret St. George	$2.99	☐
HAR#16515	NO ROOM AT THE INN by Linda Randall Wisdom	$3.50	☐
HAR#16520	THE ADVENTURESS by M.J. Rodgers	$3.50	☐
HS#28795	PIECES OF SKY by Marianne Willman	$3.99	☐
HS#28824	A WARRIOR'S WAY by Margaret Moore	$3.99 U.S. $4.50 CAN.	☐

(limited quantities available on certain titles)

	AMOUNT	$
DEDUCT:	10% DISCOUNT FOR 2+ BOOKS	$
ADD:	POSTAGE & HANDLING	$
	($1.00 for one book, 50¢ for each additional)	
	APPLICABLE TAXES*	$_____
	TOTAL PAYABLE	$_____
	(check or money order—please do not send cash)	

To order, complete this form and send it, along with a check or money order for the total above, payable to Harlequin Books, to: **In the U.S.:** 3010 Walden Avenue, P.O. Box 9047, Buffalo, NY 14269-9047; **In Canada:** P.O. Box 613, Fort Erie, Ontario, L2A 5X3.

Name: _____

Address: _____ City: _____

State/Prov.: _____ Zip/Postal Code: _____

*New York residents remit applicable sales taxes.
Canadian residents remit applicable GST and provincial taxes.

HBACK-JM2